DAUGHTER OF
SHADOWS

Daughter of
Shadows

Tiffany Putenis

CONTENTS

Chapter 1	1
Chapter 2	15
Chapter 3	21
Chapter 4	29
Chapter 5	35
Chapter 6	45
Chapter 7	53
Chapter 8	61
Chapter 9	67
Chapter 10	75
Chapter 11	81
Chapter 12	89
Chapter 13	97
Chapter 14	107
Chapter 15	115
Chapter 16	125
Chapter 17	133
Chapter 18	137
Chapter 19	145
Chapter 20	153
Chapter 21	163
Chapter 22	171
Chapter 23	179
Chapter 24	187
Chapter 25	195
Chapter 26	207
Chapter 27	217
Chapter 28	223
Chapter 29	229
Chapter 30	235
Chapter 31	249
Chapter 32	257
Chapter 33	269

Chapter 34   279
Chapter 35   285
Chapter 36   291
Epilogue   295

Acknowledgments   297
About the Author   299

For Memere, looking down on me from Heaven.
My biggest fan, and the type of woman I aspire to be:
Brave, loyal, and fiercely independent.

I love you.

CHAPTER ONE

S he couldn't remember a time when she hadn't been cold. The before times grew hazier with each day that passed, until she could no longer remember her father's smile or the scent of her mother's perfume. Someone loved her once, but the feeling was distant, diluted by the life or death struggle she faced every day in the alleys that bordered the harbor district. She no longer felt sadness at their loss, only an emptiness. The loneliness of her existence drowned her.

Sayah knew she was beautiful. She often saw her face reflected in puddles or the glass shop windows in the wealthy district of Ship's Haven and she noticed the way men looked at her when she forgot to hide herself. Large blue-green eyes that shone like aquamarines set in a heart shaped face, long black hair, and a delicate hourglass figure with a curvy derriere made her stand out amongst the crowds of people on the streets, a hazard for a young woman with no home or family to speak of and no one to protect her from those who would take her beauty for themselves. She quickly learned to hide herself behind layers of dingy fabric that obscured her form and kept her hair tightly braided and tucked into her cloak. And she used the shadows, twisting them around herself to blur her movements and quiet her steps. They acted as camouflage, hiding her when darkness fell and the devilish dandies came out to prey on the less fortunate.

She watched as the sun went down, painting the sky in deepening shades of blue as twilight descended. The last vestiges of the day's light glinted off the stained glass windows that stretched high above the nave, lining the walls of the sanctuary. They sent shifting colors across the pristine white plaster walls inside, bringing a cheerful glow to the otherwise demure church. Standing proudly in the canal district of Ship's Haven, Our Lady of Charity stood nestled between the townhouses of shipwrights, successful merchants, and politicians, visible from nearly every part of the city. The church's old stone walls had stood for millennia as its priestesses preached to the masses about the sins of wealth and the need to absolve oneself of such sins through donations and kindness. Sayah stood and stretched, her knees stiff from kneeling on the narrow wooden boards in front of the pews for hours. The padded fabric that lined them had long since lost its cushion, leaving indentations from the hard wooden edges in her skin.

That last sermon was a doozy, she thought. *I could barely—*

"Sayah, you're still here?" the priestess called from the altar, interrupting her thoughts. Long robes of the purest white clung to her curves before falling from her hips, barely brushing the tops of her bare feet with gilt lacquered toenails. Her golden hair shone, looped in and around a tiara that resembled shooting stars.

"Yes, Mother. I was deep in thought and lost track of time." Sayah rolled her shoulders back, straightening her posture and attempting to hide the small hole in her dress just below the waist. "Your last sermon was particularly well done. I truly felt the power in your words."

The priestess preened at the praise, a wide grin spreading across her face. A golden filling glinted from one of her molars. "Just as well, then, that I need help with dousing the candles and sweeping the nave," she said. "Come, take this snuffer and get started."

Sayah nodded her assent and grabbed the snuffer, walking toward the back walls to put out the candles that lined the walls and altar. She lost herself in the repetitive work, allowing her mind to drift. The scent of doused flames and sandalwood filled the air, smoke tendrils trailing behind her as she worked. The priestess smiled softly from where she knelt beside the guttering flames of four candles dancing in the molten wax. They worked in companionable silence, preparing the sanctuary for nightfall.

I wish I could hum while I worked in here, Sayah thought. *This type of work really needs a little song to keep you moving at a steady pace. But Mother doesn't approve of music in the sanctuary, though the presence of music would be a charity for people who experience great sadness in the silence.* She sighed internally. *People like me.* She sighed again, turning her mind back to the task at hand.

"Sayah," the priestess said, the broom moving swiftly between the pews, "have you considered joining the Order? With no family to care for you-"

"No," Sayah said, her voice firm. "I will not become a priestess. That isn't what is meant for me."

"We could look after you, care for you." The usually smooth skin of the priestess's brow furrowed deeply. "You are here most days, hiding amongst the pews during the devotionals. It would be no different, beyond the clothing you would wear."

Sayah sighed. *It always comes down to this*, she thought. *It is never enough to let me visit, to let me pray. It's always circled back to taking me into the order and giving me a new life, whether I remember my old one or not.* She shook her head vigorously in response to the priestess's statements.

"Mother, I know that you mean well and that you care about me, and I appreciate that. I do. But I... I can't bring myself to start a new life when I can't even remember my old one. There's too much I can't remember about my past," she said. "Too many questions that I need answers for. Answers I won't find in a sanctuary, regardless of the god or goddess worshiped there."

The priestess nodded, her face solemn. "You have never allowed us to help you in your quest for the truth. I find it hard to believe that you will learn anything at this point." A frown darkened her features. "Are you still searching for answers after all this time?"

"I will search until I finally have them. I need to understand what happened to my parents. What happened to me…" she trailed off, lost in thought.

If the priestess wondered about what happened to her, she didn't ask. She set the brooms aside and grasped Sayah's hands in hers, then walked away without another word, heading through the narrow archway that led to the priestesses' quarters. Sayah shook herself, bringing her mind back to the present, and exited the sanctuary. The sky had darkened to deep indigo while she was tucked into the pews, and the wind held a bitter bite that cut through her cloak and layered petticoats and skirts. As she stepped away from the consecrated ground of the church, she slid into the shadows and pulled them close to her, blurring her form and hiding her from sight. She stepped carefully to avoid disturbing any of the flowers and bushes that lined the cobbled street.

I should head toward The Rusty Pig, she thought as she sidestepped a puddle and dodged left, narrowly avoiding a collision with a wizened old man wrapped in a heavy wool coat. *If Bess is still there, she'll sneak me a meal, maybe a tankard of ale.*

She headed toward the tavern, deftly avoiding the barrels and heaps of trash in the dingy alleys that led toward the dock district of Ship's Haven. Nice homes gave way to ramshackle tenements, the scent of unwashed bodies and spoiling food clinging to the air. Seedy looking men wearing threadbare cloaks leaned against a lamp post, exchanging a small package in the dim light. A couple shouted at each other, their voices ringing out from a flat far above street level; the noise echoed in the short alley. A loud crash rang out, immediately followed by cursing, abruptly stopping the argument. Sayah ducked between two buildings, blending into the shadows in the narrow space. As she rounded the corner to The Rusty Pig, she stepped in something slick and slipped, falling into a stack of crates. Her shadows dissipated as the crates crashed around her.

"Dammit," she cursed under her breath. The clatter attracted attention from further down the street, and a night watchman shined his lantern toward her as she struggled to her feet.

"Are you okay, miss?" he asked, catching her elbow to steady her.

"Yes, officer," Sayah said. She shivered as the cold breeze hit her now damp skirts. The smell of fish guts and refuse permeated her clothing from the muck she'd landed in. She cursed herself and her foolishness as she watched his eyes rove across her body.

"You should be more careful. Being out here at night isn't safe," he said. "A pretty thing like you will attract a lot of unwanted attention. Unless that's what you're looking for?"

"No, sir. I was just finding my way home from helping the priestesses at Our Lady of Charity."

"Ah, an acolyte? I see." He leered at her, undressing her with his eyes. He licked his lips.

"Yes, sir," she lied, pretending not to notice the way he looked at her. "Now I must get home to my mother. She is waiting for me" She walked away, skirting around the night watchman and making a beeline for an older woman sitting out on her steps. She sat on the steps beside her, hoping the woman wouldn't react and give her away.

"Hi Mama," she said, looking up at the gray-haired woman.

The woman reached a hand out and cupped her shoulder. Sayah smiled. The night watchman raised his hand in a salute, then slung his lantern over his shoulder and strolled away, whistling. Sayah heaved a sigh of relief and stood, shaking out her damp skirts.

"Thank you," she said to the old woman.

"You're welcome."

Sayah trotted down the steps and ducked around the corner, leaning against the wall to collect herself before wrapping herself in shadows again. She stuck close to the wall, running her fingers along the crumbling bricks and carefully avoiding the shafts of light angling from the thin windows of the tenement. Ahead of her, the alley opened into a dimly lit street; music filled the air, spilling out of the windows and open door of a large building. A behemoth of a man sat on a bench beside the door, leaning against the wall with his arms crossed above his chest.

Finally, she thought. *The Rusty Pig.* She released her hold on the shadows and skirted around the building, heading toward the kitchen entrance of the tavern in search of her friend Bess. The worn wooden exterior sported peeling paint and missing window panes, but there was always a fire in the hearth and fresh kegs of ale to tap, so it remained a popular place to be.

"Get your filthy hands out of that pan, you greasy slugabed," a shrill female voice said. A piece of pottery shattered as she cursed. "Damn you for a fool, look what you've done. Gone and wrecked my best pie pan."

"Bess?" Sayah said quietly as she crept toward the door. "Don't kill the man for wanting some pie."

A delicate, oval shaped face peeked out from around the door frame, smudges of flour and cocoa smearing her cheeks and the tip of her slightly upturned nose. "Oh, Sayah. It won't be the pie he'll be dying for."

"I came to see about a meal, and maybe a tankard, if you're feeling generous. But it sounds like I should head out again, if you're planning a murder over your pie pan." Sayah smirked as she heard heavy footsteps exiting the room at a rapid pace.

"Don't be ridiculous," Bess said, swinging open the lower portion of the kitchen door to let Sayah in. "Get yourself in here. We've got a beef pie and fresh oat bread, kept warm beside the ovens, and I can have a tankard for you in a minute or two after I get these plates out to the sailors at the bar." She dished up pie and two large slices of bread thickly coated in rich butter onto a plate. "Eat. I can see you're hungry. Haven't eaten today is my guess."

Sayah's stomach growled loudly as she nodded in agreement. "Not a morsel."

"I'll be right back with that ale," Bess said as she swung out the kitchen door and into the tavern's busy taproom.

When she returned a moment later, she held a large pewter tankard in both hands. Taking a long swig from one, she set the other before Sayah on the work table that dominated the center of the room. "So why didn't you manage a meal today? That isn't like you."

"I hid out at Our Lady of Charity and got roped into sweeping and snuffing again. The priestesses don't allow food in the sanctuary, no matter how badly they want you to join them."

"They're still trying to get you to join the Order?" Bess shivered at the thought of her friend wearing the white robes and gold chains of a priestess.

"Yes," Sayah said. "But I told them unequivocally no this time. I don't think I'll be welcomed back there, regardless of the situation."

"Doubtless they will block you out. 'Our Lady of Charity,' they say. Yet they help no one but themselves." Bess spat, flinging spittle and chewing tobacco into the rusting tin spittoon by the door. She sat heavily in a worn wooden chair by the fire, putting her feet up on an overturned soup pot.

Sayah chewed thoughtfully on a bite of beef pie, gravy dripping down her chin. Rosemary and sage flavored the rich gravy. Her stomach roared its appreciation for the buttery, flaky crust and delicious filling. "You've a truly talented hand with pie crust, Bess," she said. The bubbles in the cold wheat ale tickled her throat with a refreshing sensation, washing down the pie and giving her a delightful little buzz at the edge of her senses. A hiccup forced its way from her diaphragm, startling her.

"Will you be staying the night, then, in the yard or the stables?" Bess asked, plopping another piece of pie down in front of Sayah.

"No, I'm for the dry docks," she replied, wiping her

mouth with her sleeve. "I heard there's a boat in for mainte-
nance next week with no one watching over it. I'll sneak
aboard and rest my bones on a real bed in the captain's quarters tonight."

"Really coming up in the world, aren't you?" Bess replied
with a hint of sarcasm. She wrapped a half loaf of bread in
paper and tied it up in twine, then put it beside Sayah's plate.
A pair of apples joined the bread, and a small hunk of hard,
sunset orange cheese. "Take these with you when you head
out. And the clean skirt hanging in my room; the one you're
wearing smells something awful. Can't have you starving to
death in the captain's quarters, and I definitely can't let you
back in here smelling like that. Never let it be said that ole
Bess doesn't pay her debts."

"Come on now, Bess, you know you don't owe me
anything."

"Anything but my life, you mean. I suppose that means I
have to pay a mind to keeping you inside your skin, don't it?"
Bess tried to look forbidding but only succeeded in making
Sayah laugh.

"I appreciate you, Bess," she said, the laughter suddenly
gone from her face. "I really do."

"I know, Sayah."

She began to gather up the food, tucking items into
hidden pockets sewn into her skirts and cloak. The musicians
in the other room stopped playing and a scuffle broke out.
Bess ran through the doors into the common room, brandishing her rolling pin above her head, her riotous curls
coming free from her pins at the movement. With a deep
breath, Sayah grabbed a final bite of pie and slipped out the
door, cloaking herself in shadow as she went.

The swirling shadows around her had scared her once,
when she was young and unable to control them. Now they

were a comfort, a safe place where she could hide and be protected. As she approached the main street beside The Rusty Pig, she let the shadows drop away. They were no good in brightly lit areas. She tried to blend with the crowd, keeping the hood of her cloak pulled forward, covering her hair and shielding her face. The crowd thinned as she passed the front door of the tavern, most of the men and women headed to their homes or off in search of a brothel in the opposite direction. The apothecary's shop stood empty across the way and she could see the haberdasher locking his door as she passed. She hurried, picking up her pace as the lights surrounding the tavern began to dim.

She rounded the corner toward the dry dock and headed down the sand-covered path toward the waiting boat. Its massive hull loomed before her. *A safe place*, she thought. *Maybe I'll be able to sleep tonight.* She strolled closer and brushed her hand against the painted wood. A wolf whistle rang out behind her and she startled.

"Oy, dearie," a rough voice shouted.

Frosty tendrils of fear clutched at her, forcing a chill down her spine. Sayah flicked a glance over her shoulder and saw the two men, dressed in the rough clothing of sailors and wearing at least three days' worth of beard. Their odor, that of unwashed bodies and liquor, overcame the strong fishy smell of her messy skirts, making her gag. She picked up her pace, gripping her skirts in her hands to keep them from getting caught in her sturdy boots. She ducked into an alley a few buildings down from the tavern, squeezing between a stack of crates and old, stained wine barrels.

Her breath came in sharp pants as she doubled over, wrapping the shadows around her for camouflage. She held her breath as the two toughs ran past, their boots heavy on the cobblestones.

"Why ya hiding, little girl?" one of them shouted. "We just want to have a bit of fun with ya."

"Aye, a bit of fun. You'll love what I do to ya," the other said. "I've got a rod worthy of—"

Sayah covered her ears, cutting off the sound of their voices as she peered through a hole in one of the crates before scooting further toward the wall. She crouched behind a stack of wine barrels near the back door. The burned stamp of another tavern, The Whining Wench, claimed them and let her know where she hid. The raucous crowd inside the popular tavern shouted over the din of the musicians inside, making lurid requests of the serving girls and demanding more ale. She shuddered at some of their words.

I can't believe the girls put up with this, she thought. *Pigs. All of them.* The musicians picked up a sprightly reel, and the sound of shoes pounding on hardwood floors floated out into the cool night air. She curled tighter into herself. Her ears pricked; the sound of leather soles scraping against stone approached her hiding spot. She closed her eyes and held her breath, waiting for the sound to pass by her.

Please don't let them find me, she thought. *Oh gods, please don't let them find me.*

The footsteps stopped. She peered through a gap between the barrels; a pair of dark boots waited on the other side, and she could hear him breathing as he searched for her. Her pulse pounded in her throat, choking her, and she stared toward the open space at the other end of the alley. *There has to be a way to get over there,* she thought. The heavy boots scraped against the stones again, one foot dragging slightly behind the other, heading away from her.

"Oy, Franz, the little git is here somewhere," he shouted. "She can't have disappeared."

Sayah leaned back against the stone wall and slipped, her

foot bumping into a loose stone on the ground. It careened forward, striking a barrel, and the street tough stopped abruptly and whipped his head around. Cursing her clumsiness, she slipped shadows around her feet, trying to silence her steps so she could creep forward, staying crouched within the shadows cast by the detritus that lined the alley. She paused, gauging the distance between them and looking further down the alley to calculate her chance of escaping.

In the distance, the shadows twisted, changing form until they revealed the shape of a young man with overlong brown hair and a surly expression on his face. He caught her eye and winked before throwing a rock toward the men and dashing away. She watched as the air around him blurred, distorting him until the shadows made him disappear to the common eye. The sailors chased after him, unaware that she was no longer in front of them. She tracked the blur with her eyes, studying him closely before racing in the opposite direction, clutching the shadows to her like a safety net.

CHAPTER TWO

She became a phantom, a thing of shadows, whenever fear or anxiety got the best of her. She had been driven by her fear and a desperate need to learn more about her powers and how she got them for as long as she could remember. For the first time, she'd encountered someone else like her. *Time to get some answers*, she thought. *I just have to get close enough to talk to him.* She turned up the next alley and watched the shadows twist ahead of her, tracking his movements through the anomalies she saw. They moved away from the well-kept alleys near the merchants and angled toward the harbor. The scent of rotting citrus fruit wafted on the salty breeze, gagging her as she passed between refuse piles that filled the alleys outside the sailors' hovels and brothels that lined the harbor. The sound of the waves pounded against the docks in the distance, setting the crude voices and clatter of the sailors to an ocean beat.

This is why I avoid this place, she thought as her head began to spin. *Something about it makes me sick.* She dropped to her knees as her stomach turned, threatening to spill the meal Bess had given her. The smell and familiar racket brought her back to the beforetimes, dredging up painful repressed memories of the day she lost everything.

The ship was late getting into the dock, and Mama was upset.

"He's ruined the evening already and we haven't even gotten to the theater yet," she said to Sayah as she paced back and forth near the tea shop closest to the docks.

"Mama, he will be here. He promised," Sayah said, her voice full of admiration and trust for her papa.

"Of course I will," a deep voice sounded from behind them. "I could never let my best girls down."

Sayah ran to him and leapt into his arms. He spun her in a circle and grinned at Kateryna. Her icy upset melted under his gaze and she ran to him too, gathering them both close in an embrace.

"Touching." The tall man, his scalp gleaming with sweat from the heat of the afternoon, came around the corner, followed closely by a shorter man with closely shorn black hair that seemed to absorb the sunlight. "You never told us how delicious your wife is, Andres. And your little girl…" he trailed off.

Sayah looked at her papa, confused by the sudden appearance of the man, and watched as he shifted before them, placing himself between her and her mama.

"Papa?" she asked.

"Shush, lovey, everything is ok."

Another man stepped out of the shadows around the corner and came to stand beside the first, then another, then another. They stepped closer, pushing Sayah and her family back toward the shadow-filled alley just beyond the dock entrance. One of the men shifted in and out of sight, shadowy tendrils surrounding him and shaping themselves to follow his movements.

Andres drew a blade from up his sleeve and flipped it in the air, a cocky smile on his face. "Care to dance?" he asked the men.

The shadowy figure dodged around Andres and grabbed for Sayah, his fingers digging into the sensitive skin of her upper arm. She shrieked in pain and Kateryna went wild, using her nails as a weapon, trying desperately to free her little girl. A laugh came from the alley behind them.

"What's this?" it said. "Little angel, what are you doing so far from your master?"

Kateryna shouted something, words Sayah couldn't understand, and her eyes glowed an otherworldly blue. As she chanted, a golden glow emanated from her. In the distance, Andres screamed as the short-haired man took his dagger from his hand with a whip of shadow. Flames of shadow seemed to dance around them as they struggled, Kateryna's words giving Andres strength as he engaged in hand to hand combat with his attacker.

"Mama," Sayah shrieked. "Papa!" She sobbed as she watched her father fall at her mother's feet, his dagger sticking out of his back. She closed her eyes, icy tendrils of fear wrapping themselves around her heart, and stretched for her mama, but the shadows that danced around them stretched toward her. They reached into her, latching on to her heart and her fear. She felt a warm light surround her and squeezed her eyes shut.

The shadowy figure dropped her arm like she had burned him, screaming unintelligible words and falling to the ground. Kateryna shouted in triumph and ran toward Sayah. Her eyes trained on her daughter, she didn't see the shadows that flowed toward her with preternatural grace. The tall, broad-

shouldered man moved slowly, flipping a shadow blade between his hands as he approached. His bald head shone like a beacon in the sun.

"Run, Sayah," Kateryna screamed, keeping a short leash on her own terror as she begged her child to flee.

Sayah ran, throwing herself into the tight alley between a sailmaker's shop and a tailor. She wrapped her arms tightly around her chest and ducked under a pile of torn sails and webbing, staring through gaps in the fabric. Her fear and horror made it impossible to close her eyes.

His strong fingers bit into Kateryna's neck as she struggled, her body writhing with her efforts to free herself from his grasp; the bald pated man moaned in rapture as her shimmering red lifeblood flowed down her body, staining her dress. When she was fully drained, he threw her aside and dipped his hand into her blood, spreading it across his lips and licking it from his fingers. Andres lay beside Kateryna, their blood mingling on the cobblestones and seeping into the cracks in the earth. Sayah collapsed where she was hidden, her heart breaking as the reality hit her—her parents were gone. She screamed, hysteria and grief filling her voice.

From a few streets over, voices rang out and the sound of people running came toward them. The men fled, hastily cloaked in shadows to hide them from sight. She crawled to her parents, pressing her face into her mama's shoulder, soaking the delicate fabric of her dress with tears. She curled into a ball beside them, their blood soaking into her cloak and gown, and unconsciously wrapped the shadows tightly around herself as a shield.

She shook herself, bringing her thoughts back to the present, staring blindly ahead. Unconscious tears flowed down her cheeks, her vibrant eyes red rimmed with long held, unceasing grief.

She shuddered, wrapping her arms tightly around herself as she shook with the force of her sobs. *Mama and Papa...the attack. The men using shadows to commit their dirty deeds. Mama laying in the pool of blood beside Papa, lifeless.* She tried to picture their faces when she did something clever, to remember the feel of her papa's hand in hers...

Nothing. Why did my memory of the attack return, but not the good memories? The tears began to flow anew.

CHAPTER THREE

S he sat still, curled into herself with her arms wrapped tightly across her legs. She lifted her forehead from her knees and inhaled a shaky breath. Her lips quivered as she looked around the alley.

So many similarities, she thought. *These crates and barrels offering me shelter, just the same as the torn sails and cloth that afternoon. I could be a block away or in the same spot, I have no way of knowing either way. So much has changed since then.* The snapping crack of a twig down the alley caught her attention.

Ahead of her and to the left, whorls of shadow twisted and faded, and the young man reappeared. He stood before a small door, tucked between piles of trash and empty barrels. He ran his hand through his hair, attempting to put it back in order, before knocking on the door. Sayah stilled, pulling the shadows tighter around her body to ensure that she couldn't be seen.

"Kage. You're late," said a husky, feminine voice from inside the door. "You know he won't tolerate tardiness."

"I had to double back a few times on my way here. There

was a pair of sailors on my tail in the merchant district, but I lost them." His baritone voice possessed a timbre that hinted at secrets and deeds best performed in the dark of night.

Sayah smirked at his words, trying to ignore the little pull of attraction she felt at the sound of his voice. The shadows warming with her amusement. *His name is Kage,* she thought. *That's far from a normal name. I guess it suits him.*

"Regardless, you're late. I wouldn't want to be you when he's done flaying the ungrateful hide from your back," the disembodied voice responded. "Come along."

The door opened wider and Kage walked through, removing his cloak and hat as he entered. The voice murmured something, almost purring. Sayah couldn't make out the words, but Kage's laughter, warm and intimate, rang in her ears. Something akin to jealousy set fire within her veins, and a low growl threatened to exit her throat. She crouched beside a large barrel that reeked of fish guts and whiskey, settling in to wait for Kage to leave again.

The wraith led Kage deeper into the building, the pale gray wisps that formed her shape shimmering and shifting as she glided along the thickly carpeted floor. Her curves were ample, despite being noncorporeal, and he hummed his approval deep in his throat as he followed her. The sound caught her attention and she shot a glare at him over her shoulder.

"Behave," she warned, her eyes as sharp as daggers.

The building, a pleasure house that catered to all manner of debauchery, served as a front for his father's other, less savory dealings. The brothel's infamy spread throughout Ship's Haven, ensuring that business boomed. He could hear the sounds of its mistresses and guests through the walls, pleasure and pain being shared. Peepholes were placed discretely throughout the walls at varying heights, allowing those whose pleasures leaned toward the voyeuristic the opportunity to view the lascivious pleasures of the staff as they served their clients. He caught a glimpse of someone peering through into a particularly popular room and the sound of a whip cracking echoed in the hall as they descended to his father's suite of rooms hidden far below the public areas of the building. Candles flickered in sconces on the walls, their light casting flickering shadows across the blood red silk that papered the walls.

"I see Father re-papered the walls again. Such a pity, I had grown fond of the black and gold damask," Kage said, tongue in cheek. "Another incident with the serving girls?"

"Don't be smart," Reisu said, her form shifting from gray to crimson in frustration. "It's not your place to question his actions any more than it's my place to question why you always return to us reeking of common tavern wenches and ale."

"Come now, those wenches were anything but common. There was one, Tessa she was called, with the most luscious lips and the softest pink…" He trailed off as Reisu smacked him on the shoulder. "What?"

"You're ridiculous. Stop before he hears you." She slowed as they approached the heavy iron door at the base of the spiral staircase. Raising her hand, she knocked twice in rapid succession.

The small panel at the top of the door slid open to reveal a deep crimson eye with a slitted pupil, then rapidly shut again.

"Enter," a voice boomed from inside the room.

"Go," Reisu said.

Kage opened the door and walked through, shutting it carefully behind him. "Hello, Father," he said.

"You're late." The shadows moved through the room, coalescing into human form. Dal'gon strode toward Kage and wrapped him in a hug. "Son. You smell of wenches and cheap ale."

"Father. I smell exactly as I always do. Delicious." Kage smirked, a small dimple flashing in his left cheek. "At least that's what the tavern wenches say. Why is everybody so fixated on my scent today?"

"Possibly because you didn't complete the simple task I gave you, then you show up late for our meeting, smelling of wenches and booze, and a hint of…Is that fish?" Dal'gon stared at him, anger flashing in his eyes. "Where is the knife?"

"Oh, that old thing? I had more pressing matters to attend to. It's tucked into a barrel of fish guts behind The Rusty Pig," Kage said. His head snapped back as Dal'gon's fist connected with his jaw. "What the hell?"

"A barrel of fish guts. You left the ritual knife…in a barrel of fish guts." Shadow tendrils snapped off of him and flames glinted behind his irises. "Months. We have been looking for that knife for months, and your only job was to retrieve it and bring it to me before anyone else could take it. Fish guts?"

"It was the only option available at the time. A pair of street toughs were chasing a street urchin. She was trying to hide behind a stack of barrels and wrapped shadows around herself for camouflage. I distracted them so she could get away. She's one of ours, right?"

"A girl? A street urchin?" Dal'gon's brow furrowed. "Continue."

"She was wrapped in the shadows; I could see them swirling around her, and she could see me when I was cloaked." Kage scratched at the stubborn five o'clock shadow that darkened his chin as he thought about how to explain the rest of what he had seen. "She seemed...different, somehow. Almost angelic. But she had powers like yours. Like ours."

"Kage, do you have any sisters?" Dal'gon asked.

"I mean, not that I know of, but—"

Dal'gon held up a hand, stopping him. "You do not have any sisters. I can only sire males."

"That must mean—she is something else entirely."

Dal'gon paced around the room, arms crossed, tapping his fingers against his left arm as he walked. The shadows of the room grew dim as he moved through them, absorbing their darkness into himself. "I do not know what she is, but I do have some suspicions. We need to find out. Get her here. And fetch the knife."

"How do you want me to do that?" Kage asked. "It's not like we exchanged addresses and agreed to become pen pals. I saw her once in an alley and didn't speak a word to her."

"You said she's a street urchin. Go out on the streets and start looking." Dal'gon's voice was hard, his tone leaving little room for argument.

"Yes, Father," Kage said.

"Leave me now. Find the girl." Dal'gon turned away from him, staring into the fireplace at the far end of the room. Around him, the shadows strengthened and swelled until his figure was distorted, disappearing into the night dark corner of the room furthest from the door.

Kage turned on his heel and walked away at the dismissal, exiting the room and jogging up the spiral stairs to the main area of the brothel. Suddenly feeling as though his skin was a size too small, he ran through the kitchens and fled through the alleyway door, ducking around the corner and gathering the shadows around himself.

At the far end of the alley, cloaked in shadow and tucked behind the crates and refuse from the brothel and its neighbors, Sayah stared at him.

I have to find out what he knows, she thought. *I have to find out where these powers come from.*

CHAPTER FOUR

The night air grew colder as midnight approached. The old stones of the buildings did little to hold heat, despite the warmth of the day, and Sayah's skin grew colder the longer she stayed close to the walls that were sheltering her. She had waited for Kage for hours; her back and knees ached from crouching in the shadows. She heard the door open and looked up as he exited the brothel.

She shivered as the wind picked up, staring at Kage as he maneuvered around the alley and wrapped himself in the dense shadows between two buildings. In the distance, she heard voices shouting and a woman's throaty laugh coming from the direction of the brothel. Lurid red light came through the few windows left unshuttered and the sounds of the den of flesh echoed into the night.

I should get out of here, she thought. *I need to move and find somewhere warm to bed down. I don't know if I can make it back to the ship before the crew arrives at the dry dock at dawn.* She stood and stretched, then closed her eyes and took a deep breath. Imagining the shadows wrapping tightly around her body like a warm blanket, she pulled more of them toward her. As the warm darkness of the shadows enveloped her fully, she winked out of view and began to move toward the open mouth of the alley and out toward the docks.

She ran, her skirts tied up at the waist to free her legs. As her boots pounded the stones along the docks, a warm laugh tinkled through the air. The sound reminded her of springtime and cherry blossoms.

Mama, she thought. "Mama," she shouted and ran toward the laughter.

As she approached, the woman caught her and spun her around in a circle, dizzy with delight. "Oh my love," she said. "I am so glad to see you. What have you been doing?"

"Running, Mama," Sayah said. "I can run so fast that nobody can ever catch me."

Her mama looked at her skirts, tied up out of the way, and smiled at the strong legs ending in small feet and sturdy boots. "Of course you can, lovey. Of course you can. You're just like your papa that way."

"When is Papa coming back?" Sayah asked, a child's innocence in her voice. "Is he on the big ship again?"

"Yes, love, but he should be home in a fortnight and we will be together again."

"Not soon enough," Sayah said as she ran off again. "I will run and find him and tell him that he needs to come home to us so that we can have supper and go see a play and dance in the gardens."

"Oh, lovey, I do wish you could." Her mama smiled, but her face was serious again.

Sayah knew that something big was happening, something

she didn't understand, but she wasn't sure what questions to ask or where to begin. Her mother had always been relatively closed-mouthed with regard to her papa's career as a ship-wright, and she never understood why he always went out on the ships he designed when he could stay at home with them and teach her to design ships of her own.

"Mama," she called. "Do you think Papa would teach me to make a ship?"

"Of course, darling, if you ask him."

"I will ask," Sayah said. "I will ask and he will have to stay so that he can teach me."

Her mother nodded, a small, sad smile on her face. As Sayah ran off to chase one of the young boys who worked at the docks, her mother rubbed her belly and sighed.

"I only hope that our next sweet little one has your zest for life, Sayah," her mama whispered, resting her hand on her gently rounded lower abdomen. "I only hope he or she will be as wonderful as you."

Sayah woke suddenly, hitting her head on the low wooden ceiling above the cot as she shot into a sitting position. The dream stayed with her, but the images faded slightly, becoming misty and distant. Her heart felt heavy as she remembered her mother's face for the first time in years.

"Mama," she whispered. "Oh, Mama." She curled into the fetal position, burying her head into her arms. Tears stained her cheeks and dripped off of her chin. The memory of her mother's face floated at the front of her mind: delicate chin, high cheekbones, full lips, blonde hair twisted into an intricate chignon. She remembered watching as her mother took the pins out of her hair in the evening, the heavy blonde curls falling down her back.

The boat shifted as wind picked up, the creaking of the wood reminiscent of an old man groaning. She shivered, wrapping her cloak more closely to her while she rocked back and forth. The wind howled and moaned through the port-holes and cracks between the boards. She lay on the cot, wrapped tightly in her cloak, and listened to the wind. The sound lulled her to a deep sleep, free of worries and dreams.

CHAPTER FIVE

D awn broke as Sayah snuck off the ship. The dry
dock was still and quiet, with only the sound of
seagulls in the air as they flew toward the sand-
bar. Excited squawks rang out as they dove down into the
water to catch fish that swam toward the surface. The soft
pastel sky's reflection painted the water, shimmering in the
ripples left by the waves.

It's been so long since I've seen a sunrise, Sayah thought.
*I've dwelled in the night for too long. Maybe, if I can find
Kage again, I can figure out what I am and why my parents
died.* She doubled back through the series of alleys that led to
The Rusty Pig, hoping to catch Bess before she started the
bread to rising for the day.

The top half of the door stood open despite the chill in the
morning air, and Sayah could hear Bess humming to herself
as she shuffled around the kitchen. Sayah climbed up the
short flight of stairs to the door and knocked quietly.

"Bess," she called. "Can I come in?"

A grunt answered her. She leaned forward and unlatched

the door from the inside, swinging it forward and stepping inside. The heat from the fire in the hearth and the wood ovens that lined the far wall radiated through the room, and the smell of yeast and flour permeated the air. Bess turned her head, her flamboyant red hair coiled into a tight spiral on the back of her head. Several loose strands floated loose and stuck to the damp perspiration on her neck. The heat provided a rosy glow to her cheeks that was obstructed by a smudge of flour

"Mmm," Sayah said, sniffing the air. "What's cooking?"

"Rye bread, and I'm stewing some root vegetables to go with the porridge. What can I do for ya, Sayah?"

"I think I remembered something," Sayah said, heartbreak painting the lines of her face. She sat heavily in the chair beside the fire, stretching her fingers toward its warmth. "Mama. I remember Mama."

Bess stopped kneading, her knuckles clutching the dark, seeded dough tightly. "You remember?" she asked.

"I remembered her face. It came to me in a dream. It's faded now, almost as though it didn't happen, but..." she trailed off.

"But you saw her. Your mother. What else?" Bess wiped her hands on a sackcloth towel, poured a cup of tea, and strolled over, setting it down on the table and crouching before Sayah.

"Nothing. It's all faded now, almost misty. Like a vision of something you didn't quite see, or something you only imagined." Her tears began anew and her shoulders shook from the violent torrent of emotion that ran through her. "She was so beautiful," she said between hiccuping sobs.

"Oh Sayah," Bess said, rocking forward onto her knees and pulling her into a hug.

Sayah rested her head against Bess's shoulder, taking a steadying breath and suppressing a hiccup as her tears slowed. Bess stroked her hands up and down Sayah's back, soothing her through the gentle touch. *I hope this doesn't tear her apart,* she thought. *It's taken so long for me to get through her walls enough that she'll come to me for food or help... Learning more about what happened to her family could do irrevocable damage to her.*

"Remember when we first met?" Bess asked. "You used those shadows of yours to save me from that street tough that was chasing me."

Sayah nodded, her voice failing her.

"When you picked me up from the ground and helped me to my feet, I told you that I'd owe you for the rest of my life and I meant it, Sayah. I want to help you." Bess pulled back and looked at her closely.

"I know," Sayah said, her quiet voice shaking with suppressed emotion.

"What else happened last night after you left? Other than the dream about your mother. I know that isn't all of it."

"Two men spotted me and chased me through the dock district. I wrapped the shadows around myself and hid in the alley, tucked beside the empty wine barrels on the opposite side of the Wench," Sayah said. "They hunted me and almost found me, but then I saw someone, a young man, twisting the shadows at the mouth of the alley. He threw something, distracting them from where I hid. Then he disappeared." She took a deep breath, steadying herself again. "They chased after him, thinking he was me. I hid for a while, then began to follow in the direction he went. He was like me, Bess."

"Like you. What do you mean?" Bess looked skeptical and very concerned.

"He could manipulate the shadows the same way I can, but there was something about him… A sense of knowing. I just kept thinking that maybe this is the chance I needed to figure out where my talent comes from and how I got it."

"Possibly. Did you find him again?"

"Yes, I saw him slipping into a brothel not far from here, talking to an unseen lady about his father being angry. His name is Kage. I didn't see her, but he followed her inside and stayed for hours. I waited for him to leave and tried to follow him again, but he disappeared." She sighed. "I have to try to find him again today. And while I was waiting for him, I remembered…"

She paused, wiping an errant tear from her cheek with the back of her hand. "I remembered the day they died in the attack. Mama was angry that Papa was late bringing the ship in. She kept saying that we were going to be late. We were waiting at the docks for him, near the old bakery that made hard tack and bread for the sailors. They were supposed to take me to the theater for the first time." Another hiccup shook her thin frame.

"Oh lovey," Bess said, her face stricken.

"We were waiting. Mama was pacing, talking to me, and Papa walked up behind us. He called me 'lovey' too. Mama called me Poppet when we were alone, but never in public. I remember so much now; it's like the floodgates opened with that first memory of the attack. Why was it easier to deal with their deaths when I couldn't remember anything?" she asked.

"Because not knowing lets you be numb," Bess said, gently grasping Sayah's hand. "Knowing means confronting the horror and sadness of everything you experienced. Your mind…it hid those things from you to protect you, to keep you safe."

"I suppose that's true," Sayah said. "And I'm glad I remembered some of this, really I am. But…" she trailed off, looking away and pushing loose strands of hair back behind her ears.

"But the pain is fresh and unbearable now."

"Yes." Sayah's lower lip trembled, a rising sea of emotion threatening to overwhelm her again.

"I'm so sorry," Bess said. She held Sayah's hands tightly in hers, gently stroking her thumbs against her palms.

"What do I do?" Sayah asked in a small voice, more to herself than to Bess.

"You move forward," Bess said. "That's all any of us can do. Move forward. Keep going. Even if it's hard."

"Can I stay here?"

"I can't give you one of the rooms over the stairs or Sergei will have my head, but you can share my rooms off the kitchens and…" She trailed off when she noticed the disbelief on Sayah's face. "What? Why are you looking at me like that?"

"You would share your rooms with me?"

"Why is that surprising to you?" Confusion furrowed Bess's eyebrows.

"Because I've been living on the streets for almost ten years and nobody has ever offered to help me or let me stay with them, other than the priestesses at Our Lady of Charity, and they only want me as another acolyte for their ranks. I've known you less than a year and you've befriended me and fed me, and now…I asked you to let me stay with you, and you agreed right away. You didn't even have to think about it." Sayah's hands shook as she reached for the long forgotten cup of tea on the little table next to her.

"You don't need to be alone anymore, Sayah. We are

friends, and I take care of my friends." Bess drew her in for a hug. "Now, what's the plan?"

"I need to figure out where Kage is. I need to find him and talk to him. I need to know why I can do what I do with shadows."

"Where did you see him last? In the alley near the brothel?"

"Yes, I followed him down part of the alley after he exited, but he cloaked himself and disappeared."

"Ok, so start there, right? At the brothel?"

"I was thinking of starting at the library," Sayah said. "Maybe I can find something about this type of…I don't even know what to call it. I've had it since my parents were killed, but I didn't see any signs that I was able to do anything like this before. I don't even know what it is."

"Magic. It's magic." Bess stood and walked over to the wide table where the bread dough was rising. She punched it down and separated it into balls, covering them with sackcloth and then wiping her hands on her apron.

"I don't believe in magic," Sayah said as she watched her friend busy herself stoking the fires in the stoves.

"You don't have to believe in something for it to be real. I don't believe in love, but you seem to be proof that it exists in some form."

"Why do you say that?" Sayah asked, her brow furrowed.

"Because your papa called you 'lovey' and your mama called you 'poppet,' and she was angry at the thought of your papa making you late for your first trip to the theater."

Sayah smiled slightly.

"Wait," Bess said. "How far is the theater from the street where you think your parents were killed?"

"Fifteen minutes walk, at most," Sayah said. "I don't think we would have met Papa at the docks otherwise."

"What else is around there?"

"The lyceum and library, a bakery, a few fishmongers, and two shipwrights' offices."

"You said you were going to start at the library, right? How far is it from the brothel?"

"Not far at all. Maybe a few blocks." Sayah stood and stretched, her cloak falling open as she moved to where Bess stood beside the ovens. "I'm going to start in that alley, then head back toward the library."

"Before you do that, you're going to eat, have a glass of ale, and change out of those clothes."

"I have nothing else to wear," Sayah said. "I've already had to borrow a skirt from you because of the mishap I had yesterday.

"We're of a size," Bess insisted, pulling her back toward her rooms off the kitchens. "Whether you've had to borrow something before matters not to me. You'll wear one of my dresses and cloaks for the day and I'll have yours washed by the laundress. I meant to drop your soiled skirt off to her today anyway."

Sayah followed along, understanding that Bess wouldn't stop or allow her to broach any arguments on the subject. She found herself being laced into the stays of a lovely deep green muslin dress with a coordinating sage green cloak.

"I did the embroidery myself," Bess said with pride.

Sayah looked closely at the hems of the sleeves and neckline, admiring the tiny stitching that made up the birds and flowers embroidered there. "What are these white birds?" she asked. "They're so beautiful."

"Doves," Bess said. "They represent peace. And the sprigs of lavender are because I love the flowers."

"This is the most beautiful thing I've ever worn. Thank

you." Tears sprang up in Sayah's eyes at the opportunity to wear such finery.

"I'm happy to lend it to you. Green is so lovely on you; it accentuates your eyes and makes your skin glow. Now go on, eat so you can get to the library and start trying to solve this mystery."

CHAPTER SIX

Sayah walked along the cobblestone streets leading to the theater, studying the crowd on the streets and watching the shadows for the telltale twists and swirls that would indicate Kage was there. All around her, people gossiped amongst themselves, stopping at market stalls and haggling for fresh citrus fruit from the merchant ships that had just arrived in port. A barker for the theater shouted about the newest play to be performed, opening that very evening, starring the luscious, Lavinia Martinet; Sayah smiled, remembering Lavinia's days as a serving girl at The Rusty Pig and her desire to become a famous actress.

It looks like she did it, Sayah thought. *She managed to become an actress after all.* She continued down the street as he continued his spiel, passing the theater's majestic granite facade and rounding the corner toward the Lyceum and its library. The buildings surrounding the street became larger, their brick and stone facades in better repair, as she approached the library. She climbed the worn stone steps and walked through the gothic archway that led to the tree-lined courtyard between the lyceum and library. Despite the chill in the air, the manicured lawn and gardens held a riot of colors with crushed stone pathways winding their way between flowering shrubs and bushes. Delicate shadows danced along the ground as the bright winter sun filtered through the leaves. The sunlight teased out the golden tones in her hair, and its warmth brought roses to her cheeks as she walked through the path that led to the library's massive wooden double doors.

The door to the left swung open as she approached, a wizened man bowing deeply at the waist to her as he held the door.

"Thank you, sir," she said as she walked through.

He smiled, revealing a gap from several missing teeth. "It's my pleasure, m'lady."

She started to correct him but stopped herself. *I certainly look the part today in one of Bess' nice dresses,* she thought. *No need to spoil the image for him.* She walked to the circulation desk and waited quietly as the woman seated there finished assisting another patron.

"Next," she called out.

Sayah approached the desk. "Ma'am, I'm looking for books on magical history. Could you please point me to the right location?" she asked.

"Magical history," the librarian said, tapping her fingers on the desk. "Reference books or fiction?"

"Reference," Sayah replied.

"Four aisles to the right and ten rows back from here," the librarian said. "Though there aren't many books on the subject. The few who do believe in magic haven't had much need to pass on their knowledge."

"I… oh, okay. Thank you for your help." Sayah looked around, counting the aisles and rows as she tried to locate the correct spot.

"To the left," the librarian said, noticing her confusion. "There's a reading table with a stained glass lamp in the center of that particular row."

"Thanks," Sayah said bashfully.

She walked to the left, counting the aisles as she passed through. When she saw the table and lamp, she paused and removed her cloak, draping it across the back of the tufted armchair beside the table. Walking to the stacks, she wandered along the shelves, trailing her fingers across the spines of the books as she studied their titles.

"*The History of Magic. Magical Beings. Demons and Thralls. Lost in Shadow. A Study of Magic. Angelic Influence: Magic in Humanity,*" she read aloud to herself as she paced. She grabbed *Lost in Shadow* from the shelf. "Hopefully, this will give me something I can use."

The tufted armchair cradled her as she settled into its cushions; a small cast-iron foot stove filled with smoldering coals and bricks sat beneath the reading table, producing just enough heat to warm the immediate area. The butterfly patterned stained glass lamp cast an aura of light around the chair and table, its blues and purples glowing softly. Sayah curled her feet under herself and draped her cloak around her like a blanket, snuggling in with *Lost in Shadow*.

"Little is known of those who can manipulate shadows," she read. *"Those abilities are rumored to be linked directly to the presence of demonic blood in a family's line. Studies of the few individuals who did not go mad as the result of their abilities were inconclusive, as demon genetics in one's history are not traceable through any scientific method currently available. It is suspected that those who did not go mad may have other genetic anomalies that allow them to sustain their exposure to the shadows while maintaining their humanity."*

She set the book down on her lap and stared at the

shelves. "The few individuals who did not go mad..." she trailed off. "The shadows can make people go mad?" She picked up the book and continued reading, a small crease forming between her delicate eyebrows.

"Of the six subjects who agreed to be interviewed regarding their abilities, two maintained their humanity and kept their sanity, despite the near constant exposure to the shadow realm. The other four began to suffer delusions around their fifth year of exposure to the shadows, eventually disappearing fully into the shadow realm. Nothing is known of the shadow realm or where it is located, but those who disappeared fully were never seen or heard from again." Sayah read for a few more minutes, becoming distracted as the subject matter in the book became dry. The author began to dissect a variety of statistics, and she found that she could no longer focus on the material as it began to exceed her mathematical knowledge. She shook herself awake as she felt her eyelids beginning to slide closed.

Five years. The people who went insane lost their minds around five years after their abilities manifested, eventually disappearing fully into the shadow realm. I started being able to manipulate shadows almost ten years ago. It must be safe for me now; I'm one of the few who is able to remain in our realm without going insane from the lure of the shadows. She sighed, then skimmed through the book a bit more in hopes of learning about where the ability comes from, but there was nothing pertinent in the slim volume. She pushed her cloak aside, throwing it over the arm of the chair, and stood, shaking out her skirts and stretching. She replaced the book, running her fingers over the spines of the books and perusing the stacks for a few more moments before deciding to head back out to begin her search for Kage.

Sayah wrapped her cloak around her shoulders again,

fastening it with the delicate fern shaped pen that Bess insisted she use, swearing that it was intended to be used with the cloak. As she passed the circulation desk, she looked for the librarian to thank her, but the desk was empty and the small lamp switched off. The light streaming in through the windows glowed golden, the bright sunlight shimmering through the leaded glass panes. She pushed the heavy wooden door open and slipped through into the daylight. She tucked her cloak a little tighter around her as a breeze kicked up, lifting its edges and sending a blast of chilled air under it and through the muslin of her dress.

She shivered and adjusted her clothing as she walked through the shrub-lined path, pulling the cloak tighter around herself to try to trap her body heat as she exited the courtyard and headed back toward the dock district. As she approached the alley where she waited for Kage the night before, she saw something. A twist of shadows in the distance gave her a glimpse of tousled brown hair and an impish smile. *Kage,* she thought. She ducked into the alley and wrapped herself in shadow, following determinedly in pursuit of the boy.

The swirling shadows appeared again at the far end of the alley, dissipating in the light that angled between the buildings. He walked ahead of her, dressed in dark pants and a tan jacket, the collar of his ivory shirt open at the throat. His cravat hung loose. He brushed his hair back from his forehead, then ran his hands through in an attempt to tame it. He looked around, as though he felt her eyes on him, then turned and stared in her direction. His golden eyes appeared to flicker with hidden fire as he caught her eye. With a smirk and a wink at her, he ran into the crowd that had formed around the buskers performing outside the theater.

I lost him again, she thought, feeling sorry for herself. She released the shadows from around herself and exited the alley, joining the crowd that stood in the street, watching a rowdy band of contortionists as they performed. *But now I know that he comes to this area often. He has to live around here somewhere.* She giggled as one of the contortionists flipped from the top of a pyramid, landing in a split on the ground before the other performers.

Sayah returned to the Lyceum and library every day for weeks. She picked her way through a wide selection of books on magic of all kinds during the daylight hours, finding little to help her discover more about the origins of her powers. In the evenings, she haunted the streets around the theater and school in desperate determination to discover where Kage was hiding. The air turned cooler as fall progressed into winter and she wandered from the Lyceum to the dock district every evening, wrapped in a tightly woven cloak of shadows. The smell of wood smoke and drying leaves filled the air in the district that surrounded the Lyceum, the scents teasing her with half-formed memories surrounded by fog. As night fell on Ship's Haven once more, Sayah turned around, trudging back toward The Rusty Pig and her shared rooms.

CHAPTER SEVEN

K age wove through the crowd of people outside the theater, his awareness of the girl prickling at the back of his mind. He knew she would search him out again, just as he'd known his father would demand that he capture her so that he could investigate how she got her powers. He quickly ducked between a carriage house and its stables, ensuring that he was unable to be seen from the crowd. He watched as she stood amongst the other spectators, watching the contortionists perform tricks that were sure to dazzle the eyes of the crowd. As one woman, small with gilded ivory skin and dark slanted eyes, twisted her body into a basket to be lifted by a man with obscenely large biceps, he concentrated on the girl, measuring the distance between them.

About 100 feet, he thought, smirking to himself. *If I can stay hidden within the shadows and use them to enhance my speed, I can wrap and grab her before the crowd notices anything is amiss.* He stalked forward, peering around the corners of the carriage house and stable to see if anyone was around who could catch him. *Damnit. One of the watchmen is coming this way. I'll have to wait.* Shadows swirled around him.

The watchman strolled by, swinging his billy club and whistling as he patrolled. He checked the alley as he passed, catching a small movement beside a low wooden crate. He jumped, startled, and shook his head slightly. "Damn rats," he muttered. "Always sneaking around and startling me on my rounds."

Kage watched as the watchman strolled away, still swinging his club, waiting for him to get a good distance away before releasing the cloak of shadows that swirled around him and sneaking back into the crowd. He walked closer to where the buskers were performing, searching for the girl. Applause erupted around him as the performers finished their performance with a flourish. The small woman scaled a pillar and flipped from the top of it, landing on the man's shoulders to thunderous applause and shrieks of excitement from the crowd. Kage looked around, searching for fair skin and golden brown hair wearing a green dress, but she was nowhere to be seen.

"Dammit," he muttered. He walked back in the direction of his father's place, hoping for a glimpse of twisting shadows surrounding a pretty girl in an alley or along a side street.

Sayah stood on the threshold of the library again, the noise of the buskers' crowd floating into the courtyard on the wind. She steeled herself and walked back into the library, bypassing the circulation desk with a nod to the clerk as she headed straight for the aisle and row she needed. She grabbed the book about demons from the shelf, thinking of the otherworldly light she had seen in Kage's eyes when he winked at her. She settled herself into the armchair once more, arranging her cloak and skirts around her before curling up with her feet beneath her and opening the book.

Demonic power would make sense, she thought, *and it could explain how I developed my abilities after the attack on my parents.* She flipped through the pages, searching for something, anything, that was related to demons who could manipulate shadows. Finally, about two hundred pages in, she found something.

"Of the minor demons, Dal'gon is best known for his ability to control shadows and bend them to his will," Sayah read. *"He is approximately 500 years old at the time of this printing. Tales of his abilities have become part of the mythology of several different sociological groups, leading this author to believe that he has traveled extensively, possibly dwelling on multiple continents and amongst a variety of cultures.*

"Common elements amongst the myths involving him include his desire to disrupt those who he feels have wronged him in some way. He is frequently mentioned as having disciples who perform his bidding and serve as conduits for him to strengthen himself. Dal'gon is also believed to have had a significant impact on history in several cultures through his disruption of trade routes and monarchies, resulting in several major wars. Despite his fondness for meddling in human affairs, Dal'gon is not known to have sired any heirs, either demon or otherwise.

"Little is known about the extent of Dal'gon's abilities with shadow manipulation. The majority of information that is accessible is anecdotal, at best, and does not possess the level of detail needed to truly analyze his abilities. It is suspected that he can use shadows to cloak himself and

others from view, as well as silencing the area surrounding him. If this information is accurate, it is reasonable to assume that Dal'gon has been part of several assassinations in past centuries, as well as a number of kidnappings and thefts."

Sayah sat back in the chair, using her hand to hold her place in the book while she digested what she read. Chewing on her lip, she turned back to the front of the book to determine when it was written.

"Three hundred years ago... but how is that possible," she whispered. "Is Kage... Dal'gon?" She flipped through the pages, searching for an illustration or some sort of description that could help her identify him. As she reached the end of the section on Dal'gon, she sighed. "Nothing."

"Do you always talk to yourself?" a deep voice asked from the stacks behind her.

Sayah jumped, the book falling from her lap and upending the small heater. She scrambled to set everything back to rights before turning around to search for the voice.

"Okay, so maybe you talk to yourself. But are you always this jumpy too? It's like you haven't been looking for me." Kage stepped around the shelves behind her, his hair rumpled as though someone had been running their hands through it.

She looked at him, arching an eyebrow in an attempt to appear unphased. "And you are?" she asked.

"Oh, I think you know exactly who I am, little girl," he said. He leaned forward, picking up the book from where she'd set it on the table. "Demons, huh? Not exactly typical reading for young females."

Sayah stared at him, flabbergasted. "What?"

"Let's not waste time playing games. I know you've been searching for me, and I know what you can do."

"Okay, if we're not playing games...who are you, really?" Sayah asked, unconsciously tightening her cloak around herself.

"I'm Kage," he said, holding out his hand, "and I'm sure you noticed me saving you from those houligans the other night, so I know that you know I can manipulate shadows, just like you can."

She stared at him, her blue-green eyes taking in his features: firm, slightly plump lips, chiseled nose and cheekbones, golden amber eyes with a hint of fire behind them. An altogether pleasing face, when she considered it carefully. "Yes, I know you saved me. I was looking for you so that I could thank you."

"No," he said, smirking. "You were looking for me because you want to know where your powers came from and why you can manipulate shadows too. You're looking for answers, not an opportunity to show gratitude."

She stopped, her breath caught in her throat. *He knows. How could he possibly know?* she thought. *What am I going to—*

"Hush," he said. He pulled the lamp's chain, plunging the area into shadows as he took a step toward her. The corner of his mouth quirked up as she stepped backward and ran into the large wooden bookshelves behind her. He pinned her against them, keeping the hard muscle of his body pressed tightly against hers; his hand came over her mouth and he stared deeply into her eyes. "Mmm," he mumbled, his pupils dilating as he studied her face.

Her heart skipped a beat at the feel of his body against her, and confusion wracked her senses. *More,* her heart seemed to call. *Please.*

His eyes darkened as though he sensed her capitulation, fiery twin flames glimmering behind his pupils, and he grabbed her wrist, pinning it above her head. He silenced her with a gag of shadows ripped from the depths of the shelves, wrapping the remaining shadows tightly around both of them to hide them from view. She struggled against him, panicked, and he pressed his hips into her to keep her still while he wrapped shadowy bindings around her wrists to trap them together. He chuckled as she glared at him, her eyes cursing him, bringing a smirk on his lips. Picking her up bodily, he threw her over his shoulder and fled from the library into the early evening air.

CHAPTER EIGHT

ayah squirmed, testing the strength of the bindings around her wrists and ankles. Darkness surrounded her. Different than the shadows she was used to, this darkness felt strange and more complete. Impenetrable. She stretched her senses, reaching for the shadows she could feel just out of reach, but they didn't respond to her.

"Tut, tut, tut," Kage said, his voice floating to her in the sea of darkness. "Silly girl, you can't manipulate shadows here. The shadow realm belongs to Dal'gon, and only those he imbues can use their powers here."

"Dal'gon," she whispered. She squirmed again, twisting her wrists from side to side in a desperate attempt to loosen the ties. "The shadow realm."

"Just the fact that you're still conscious is amazing," Kage said, his voice tinged with amusement. "Most mortals would have passed out by now. The unending darkness of the shadow realm tends to be…less than hospitable." He snapped his fingers and a deep purple light surrounded them. "What are you, little girl?"

"I don't know," Sayah said. "I just… that's why I was

looking for you. I knew that you can do what I do, and I wanted to figure out what it is and why I can do it."

"'It,' as you so eloquently put it, is shadow manipulation, and I have no idea why you can do it," he said with an edge of sarcasm. He leaned closer to her. "Why do you think I have any answers for you?"

"Listen, I don't know, I just saw you that day. All I've wanted to know is how this happened to me and how I can get rid of it. I don't want it." Tears slid down her cheeks, the iridescent trails of their descent glimmering in the dim purple light. She pulled against the bonds again, struggling to free herself before finally going limp. Her head dropped forward and a low sob escaped her throat. "I just want to be normal."

"You'll never be normal," Kage said bluntly. "This ability is not something you can get rid of. Something in your blood calls to me, calls to the shadows, like a beacon of light from a lighthouse calls to a ship."

Sayah stared at him in the dim light. The light flickered, casting dancing shadows across Kage's face. Her eyes lingered on his full lips, and her own lips parted. He smiled, the corners of his mouth curving upward as he noticed her studying him.

"Like what you see?" he asked. He pressed closer, feeling her body tense against his as her pupils dilated.

"Um," she said, her eyes wide. She licked her lips. "No?"

He laughed, pulling back from her and running a hand through his hair. He grabbed her bindings and pulled her forward, pushing her out of the shadow realm and back into reality. They stepped forward into an elegantly furnished bedroom with deep red silk wall coverings. Intricate carvings decorated the heavy mahogany canopy bed and shimmering, diaphanous curtains hung from its posts, swaying slightly in the breeze that came in from the high windows. Sayah looked around the room in disbelief as the shock of candlelight after near total darkness began to wear off.

"Where are we?" she asked Kage.

"This is my father's home," he replied as he led her to the bed. He secured her wrists to the wrought iron on the headboard.

"Your father's home."

"Yes. My father's home. As in where he lives?"

"I understand that. But why bring me here?" Her brow furrowed, concern darkening her eyes.

"He wants to meet you. And he may have the answers to your questions, if you survive the meeting."

"If I survive?"

"You'll see." Kage walked to the door and looked back over his shoulder. "Don't go anywhere." A smirk teased the right corner of his mouth in amusement at his quip. He released the shadows binding her and walked out of the room, locking the door.

Sayah stretched, rubbing her wrists where the bindings had pressed into her skin, marring her pale skin. She stood, stretching her legs before walking toward the door and testing the lock.

"Damn," she muttered. "He did secure it." She tried to twist a shadow into the lock, but it resisted her. She tried again, staring at the knob and focusing intently. "Ugh," she exclaimed as her head began to pound from effort. "I give up." She walked to the armoire in the corner of the room, turning the key left in the lock. As the door swung open, a ball fell out, bouncing across the room before rolling under the bed.

She peered into the armoire, looking through the toys and books that were stored there. A light layer of dust covered the majority of the items. She opened a leather-bound tome, remarkably clean of dust, with a heavily worn binding and touched the engraving on the inside of the cover.

"Kage," she read, studying the childish scribbles on the inner cover. She closed the book gently. "This was his room when he was a child." She carefully returned the book to its shelf inside the armoire and closed the door again, twisting the small key in the lock. Silence surrounded her; not even the echo of people in the alleys and streets entered through the windows. She paced around the room, feeling like a wild animal trapped in a cage.

CHAPTER NINE

Kage descended the spiral stairs deeper into the house, searching for his father. Reisu was nowhere to be found, and the brothel was eerily quiet as he traversed the halls in search of them both. One of the ladies peered around the corner as he passed, fear plain on her face.

What the hell is going on? he wondered. *Father and Reisu are always here, and Reisu is never far from the girls. Someone has to keep them in line.*

As he got deeper into the bowels of the house, the air chilled and the smell of meat roasting filled the stairs.

"Father?" he called out as he stepped off the staircase and into the vestibule before his father's suite.

A flicker of gray flashed in the corner of the room and Reisu materialized. Her spectral form shifted and curved as the light from the candles along the massive marble mantle reflected against her, highlighting the wisps of smoke that formed her body.

"Kage," she said, surprise in her voice. "What are you doing here?"

"Looking for my father," he replied, looking at her

steadily. "I have the girl. What are you doing in my father's suite?"

"We were having a discussion regarding a…situation with one of the ladies upstairs," she said coolly. "You have the girl?"

"Yes, I found her in the library at the Lyceum, of all places." He shrugged. "She was searching for me, too. I have her restrained upstairs, waiting. Where has my father run off to?"

"He's within, in his bedroom," Reisu said nonchalantly. She strolled out of the antechamber, flicking a quick glance at him over her shoulder, then wandered up the spiral stairs and out of view.

Kage looked down. *A situation. Right.* He shook his head in chagrin, then walked to the elegantly carved door and knocked twice in rapid succession.

"Enter."

Here we go, he thought. He took a deep breath and twisted the knob, stepping through into the room. The candle-light was dim, with only a few candles lit on the bedside tables that cast twilight shadows around the room as they flickered. Dal'gon lounged in the rumpled sheets covering the massive bed, the thin, black silk top sheet curled sinuously across his lap. The long waves of his raven black hair were mussed, tendrils of shadow shifting in and out of the messy strands in the flickering light.

"Father," Kage said. "I have the girl."

"And yet you didn't bring her to me?" One dark eyebrow arched high toward his hairline. "Where is she?"

"Up-upstairs," Kage stuttered. The old fear his father instilled in him snuck up, threatening his devil may care atti-tude as he felt the judgment and anger in that simple eyebrow raise. "I se-secured her in my…"

"Stuttering again? I thought you were past that ridiculous issue. What were you able to learn about her?"

"She's stubborn and strong," Kage said. "She doesn't seem to be afraid of me, just angry that I caught her when she was trying to find me. Her ability to manipulate shadows is primitive but well-honed. She doesn't know what it is or where it came from."

"And you believe that?"

"I do. The technique she uses is different from ours, but it seems to achieve the same results. I don't think she learned from one of your disciples."

"Interesting. If not one of my disciples, then who?" A crease formed between his eyebrows. "Something I'll have to ponder. Have you given more thought to how we can use her?"

Kage looked at Dal'gon, confusion in his eyes. "I wasn't aware that you intended to use her for anything," he said. "What possible use could she have?"

"If she has the ability you say she does, she could be useful in our plans. If not, we can't have her roaming free with those powers. Either way. Bring the girl to me. Unless you would rather I come to her?"

Kage nodded and straightened, adjusting his posture. He turned and walked to the door. "I'll bring her to you within the hour."

"I'll hold you to that," Dal'gon said as he walked to the door.

Kage left, ascending the stairs and wandering through the halls back to Sayah and his childhood bedroom.

～

She sat in the center of the large bed, her knees drawn up under her chin. Kage had been gone for what felt like hours, and she had explored every inch of the room. Exhaustion sank in and she rested her forehead on her knees, the petticoats and skirts of her dress pillowing her head. She let her mind drift as she curled into herself, her breathing becoming the slow rhythm of sleep.

Mama lifted her, twirling her in a circle before nestling her close. Sayah's legs wrapped around Mama's waist and she tucked her face into her neck, inhaling the scent of jasmine and tuberose from her soap. She nuzzled close, resting her head and listening to her mama's heartbeat.

Tears formed in her eyes as the emotion of the memory hit her. She snuffled, biting back a sob as she hugged herself tightly. The door latch clicked and the door swung open. Kage walked in, closing the door behind him.

"What? What's wrong?" he asked.

"N-nothing," she said, her voice thick with unshed tears.

"Doesn't sound like nothing."

"Just a memory. I'm fine. I'll be fine."

"A memory of what?"

"My mother," Sayah said, wiping her eyes with the back of her hand. "She and my father were killed when I was little. I was with them when it happened."

"Oh. Um…" He trailed off sheepishly, unsure how to respond.

"You don't need to say anything." She frowned slightly, the movement of her lips allowing another tear to slip free. "That's the day I found out I could manipulate shadows, though. The men who attacked us…one of them used shadows to inflict invisible wounds and drain the blood from my parents without leaving a mark." She paused, taking a steadying breath. "I watched him as he dropped my mother's body to the ground beside my father's. Like it was trash. Like she didn't mean anything. Like they didn't matter."

"He used shadows," Kage said, narrowing his eyes.

"Yes," she said. "Mama told me to run, so I was hiding beneath torn sails and cloth outside the sailmaker's shop in the alley. The man, he just…disappeared, then reappeared out of the shadows behind my papa, wielding a spear of shadow that disappeared when the sunlight hit it. He stabbed the spear toward Papa and he fell to the ground, and the other men rifled through his pockets while the bald man chased down and attacked my mother."

Kage paced in front of the bed as she spoke. "Bald man? What did he look like? Can you describe him?" he asked.

"Tall and thin, about your height. He was bald and younger, maybe mid-twenties. It was so long ago, and I was so scared… The others were shorter, and one was stout and round like a keg of ale." She stopped, trying to remember more.

"My height, thin, bald," Kage repeated. He studied her closely, trying to discern how much she was hiding from him. "And one was short and stout."

She nodded. "I can't remember much else right now. I only remembered all of this a few days ago, after that night near The Rusty Pig. The memories…they've been returning in fits and spurts ever since."

"I see," he said. "That is interesting. And you manipulated the shadows for the first time that day?"

"I ran to Mama and Papa where they lay on the ground and laid next to them. I don't even remember what I did or how I did it that time. It was like a master weaver with a loom; I wove the shadows around myself and lay beside them, wishing I would die. I don't know if the ability was there before or if I got it that day." Tears fell from her chin as she began crying in earnest. "When I woke up after crying myself to sleep, I ran and hid in a pile of empty crates behind a bakery. There was so much blood on my clothes that my skirt was stiff and brown in spots. I don't even remember what color it was before…my whole memory of that day is of blood flowing from my mother and cowering behind crates. I've been on my own since." She hiccuped, then curled more tightly into herself, squeezing her arms tight around her knees.

Kage didn't know what to say. Her pain was palpable, filling the room with its presence.

The man she described… he sounds so familiar, and that trick he did with the shadows. Only one person could have taught someone how to do that: Dal'gon. Could the attackers have been some of his disciples? He stopped pacing abruptly. *Maddox,* he thought. *Big brother, what have you done? And the stout one… Could that be Damon? Father has never trusted him to go out on his own, so it makes sense that he would have gone out with Maddox for such a mission.*

He walked to the bed and sat down beside her. "What's your name?" he asked. "I never asked you for your name."

"Sayah," she replied, looking at him. Her brow furrowed slightly. "I'd tell you my surname but…I don't remember it." In the distance, a clock began to chime the hour.

"My time is up," Kage said. "My father will be coming to meet you soon, since I didn't bring you to him within the hour."

"Your father. Dal'gon is your—"

"Yes," he said calmly.

"You're half demon." Shock drained the color from her face and she edged backward to get away from him.

"Not by choice," he said.

"And your father is the shadow demon, the one who I was reading about when you—"

A knock on the door startled them both, and Sayah held her breath. The beat of her heart pulsed in the hollow between her collarbones.

"Enter," Kage said.

CHAPTER TEN

D al'gon strolled through the door, shadows licking off of him like flames. His skin shifted between the myriad colors of twilight before settling to a golden tan.

Sayah slid to the edge of the bed and stood, straightening her skirts and drawing herself up to her full height. She looked him up and down before staring into his golden eyes. *Just like Kage's*, she thought, *Dangerous, like rye whiskey, and just as potent.*

Kage instinctively took a half step forward, positioning himself between Sayah and his father. "Hello, Father," he said.

"It's been well over the hour you promised, Kage," Dal'gon said, his deep voice reverberating with whispers of darkness and betrayal. His eyes lingered on the delicate features of Sayah's face, then dipped lower. "Now, who is this lovely creature?"

"Sayah," Kage said, holding his hand out in her direction.

Sayah stared ahead, unyielding, but she accepted Kage's hand and moved to stand beside him. She looked back and forth between them. Dal'gon seemed familiar, in some way, but she couldn't place how. Kage looked a lot like him, but that wasn't it. There was something in his face that reminded her of someone she had seen once.

"Sayah," Dal'gon said. "What a beautiful name. It means 'shade,' does it not?"

"I don't know, sir. I've never looked it up."

"Your parents didn't tell you the meaning of your name?"

"My parents were killed when I was a young girl," she said with ice in her voice. "I'm sure there were many things they had hoped to tell me when I was older. They weren't given the chance."

"I see." Dal'gon's face remained impassive, but a flicker of something flashed in his eyes. "Thank you for your candor, Sayah. I am certain it was not easy to lose parents so young." He quickly turned his gaze toward Kage. "Son. I shall expect you to visit me in my suite later this evening, once you've gotten our...guest...situated."

"Yes, Father. I will come find you later." Kage's eyebrows furrowed. He opened his mouth again to speak, but stopped himself.

"I'll see myself out," Dal'gon said. "Pleasure meeting you, Sayah."

She nodded at him, struggling to find her voice to speak. As his father exited the room, Kage closed the door behind him and secured the lock. He wove a network of shadows across the door to prevent eavesdropping, then turned to stare at Sayah.

"The man you described earlier, the tall one," he said. "His name is Maddox. The short, stout one is Damon."

"How do you know that?" Sayah asked, confusion mingling with frustration in her voice.

"Because there is only one person I know who can do

those things with shadows: my father. And Maddox is his oldest child. My brother, the favored disciple."

"Your brother." She stared blankly at the wall. "You're saying—"

"I'm saying that I think my brother and two of my father's other disciples killed your parents. I'm saying that I think my father may have had them killed."

"Other disciples," she repeated, a dazed look on her face. "But why? Why would he do that? They weren't a threat."

"I don't know," Kage said. "But Maddox only kills on Father's orders. One of your parents was involved in something. Something that my father didn't want going on."

Sayah sat down heavily on the bed and buried her face in her hands. Intense emotion bubbled to the surface and sobs shook her body.

"I just—"

"Don't," she said. Tears thickened her voice, but there was ice in her eyes as she glared at him. "Don't tell me how sorry you are. Don't stand there and lie to me. You're their family. You're part of their organization."

"I—"

"Stop. Just stop."

"For the gods' sake, woman, will you let me finish a damn sentence?"

"Your family killed my family. I have been alone, living on the streets with nowhere and no one to turn to. No safety, no comfort. Nothing. Because of your father and brother." She picked up a vase from the bedside table and flung it at him. "I had to watch them bleed out and die. I lost everything. There is nothing you can say. Nothing."

He dodged the vase and jumped away as the delicate porcelain shattered against the wall. He held his hand out, palm facing her. "Sayah, stop. Please."

She threw herself face down on the bed, her body wracked with hysterical sobs.

"Sayah," he whispered, sitting beside her on the bed. He gently touched her back.

Sayah pulled away, curling into the fetal position and tucking her face against her knees. She wrapped her arms around her head to block him out. He sighed and stood up, throwing the quilt from the foot of the bed over her. As he exited the room, he turned back to look at her.

"I know this is hard, and I know you don't trust me. But I didn't know. I'll be back in the morning."

Kage flung open the door to his father's rooms, not bothering to follow protocol and knock. He strode in, his face hot with anger and shame.

"Did you know?" he shouted, slamming the door behind him. "Did you know that you killed her parents?"

"Just jumping into it, then? Okay." Dal'gon smirked from the settee across from the fireplace. "If you want to be completely accurate, I didn't kill her parents. Maddox did."

"And we both know who controls Maddox and the other disciples, don't we?" Kage spat at his father, eyes narrowed. "Maddox wouldn't dare twist a shadow without your permission."

"Do you truly hold your brothers in such low regard? They are quite capable of making their own decisions, you know. Maddox just chooses to do what I ask, when I ask it, because he understands what you've always had trouble with."

"And what is that?" Kage asked, venom filling his voice.

"That I'm a demon, one of the most powerful beings in

the world, and you, my boy, are here at my whim. I brought you into creation, I gave you power, I decide how you live… and when you die." The threat hung in the air between them, as sharp as a knife to the gut. "You have nothing unless I allow it."

"I—" Kage cut himself off, staring down his father. Angry color filled his cheeks and the flames behind his irises ignited.

"Shall we discuss my opinion of your little waif?" Dal'gon asked.

"My little waif? That's rich," Kage scoffed. "She isn't mine in any way. Why would you think I care enough about her to want to know your opinions?"

"Because, son, you do have a knack for self-preservation. She is quintessential to my future plans, and if you want to keep her, and yourself, alive, we're going to figure out how she managed to manifest shadow powers without any demon blood." Dal'gon wandered over to the sideboard and poured himself a large glass of deep red wine. He swirled the liquid around the glass and held it to his nose, inhaling the bouquet of cherries and chocolate that lingered just below the surface. Smiling slightly, he took a sip. "Would you care for a glass?" he asked.

Kage didn't answer, just walked over, picked up a cut glass decanter of scotch, and popped the top free. He took a deep swig straight from the decanter, then walked to the leather wing chair beside the fire and rested the bottle on his leg.

"Okay," he said. "Let's talk. What do you mean 'without demon blood'?"

"You mean you haven't figured out what she is yet?" A smile twisted Dal'gon's face and the flames behind his irises shone brighter, like a stoked fire on a cold day.

CHAPTER ELEVEN

She woke as the sun rose, the pale sunlight watery as it shone through the windows, still wet with morning dew. Her eyes felt gritty and the bright light made her head ache. A quick glance in the mirror on the dresser revealed dark red rims around her eyes and the salty trail of tear stains down her cheeks.

"Lovely," she mumbled as she rubbed her eyes with her hands in a desperate attempt to remove the grit. She stood and walked over to the window, looking out over the rooflines of the dock district.

At this distance, the ocean looks like glass, she thought. *It's been so long since I got to see a view like this. Not since I climbed to the top of the tower at Our Lady of Charity. This is...different, somehow.* She leaned against the window frame and rested her head against the cool glass.

There was a light knock on the door followed by the hinges creaking as someone slipped into the room.

"What are you doing here, Kage?" she asked without turning around.

"It is my room," he said, his voice dripping with sarcasm.

"But I told you I would come back in the morning. So here I am."

"I want to leave." She turned to face him.

He felt an unfamiliar ache as he saw the damage left behind by the torrent of tears the night before. "I would like you to stay," he said plainly. "I would like to help you."

"Pity the poor waif, huh? Poor little Sayah, orphaned by your brother." She shook out her skirts and straightened. "I don't want your pity."

"No, you don't. But you do want to know how you got your abilities. I want to help with that."

"And if I don't want your help?"

"You know you do. You were searching for me in the market and by the Lyceum."

"That was before I knew," she said with venom in her voice. "How could you think I would ever want your help now?"

"Because," he said, trying to keep his voice calm and rational, "my father may have given me our first clue regarding your abilities last night without meaning to."

She raised an eyebrow in his direction, doubt written plainly across her face.

"Until you, the only people who had power over the shadows had one huge thing in common," Kage said. He sat on the edge of the bed and gestured for her to join him.

Sayah sat on the floor near the window, leaning back against the wall. "And what's that?" she asked. "The ability to be a horrible person?"

"No," he said, "but I see where you're coming from. All of us are sons of Dal'gon. The results of his affairs with the lovely ladies of Ship's Haven and other port cities around the globe. Except you."

"I'm not—"

"No. He had no idea you existed. You're not one of his progeny."

"If not, then what? What am I?"

"That's what I'm not sure about. If you aren't part demon, you should have no magical ability whatsoever, especially over shadows. The only other being as powerful as a demon that I can think of is—"

"An angel."

"Yes," Kage said.

Sayah stared, not registering anything around her. *Mama,* she thought, not realizing that she said the word aloud. The memory of her mother glowing as she chanted words in a language Sayah didn't understand floated to the forefront of her mind. *Glowing. Like an angel. Like someone with power.*

"I think—I think maybe my mother had power," she said after several minutes of silence. "The day they died, she was chanting. While your brother held her by the arms, she was shouting words at him in a language I didn't know. Her skin... it glowed."

"Glowed," he repeated. "Your mother glowed?"

"I didn't remember much of that day until recently, and even then, I thought that was a figment of my imagination. But maybe... I don't know. Maybe she had power." Sayah was shell shocked, completely unable to process that information.

Kage sat still, watching her as she worked through the facts that sat before her. *Father was right,* he thought. *She had no idea what she was. Neither did I, though I suppose the description of her as a lighthouse to a ship is relatively accurate. Maybe it's not so much that she can use the shadows as her being able to bend the light in such a way that she can use the resulting shadows to her benefit. Or maybe—*

"Kage?" she whispered.

"Yes?"

"You just went blank. Like you were here but not actually here," Sayah said, a tiny furrow forming between her eyebrows.

"Sorry, I was thinking," he said. "I got a little lost in my thoughts."

"It's fine, she said. "I don't think I was all here, either. So you think I'm… an angel?"

"At least part angel. It would explain a lot."

"Like what?"

"Like why I'm drawn to you like a moth to a flame," he said without a hint of guile. "Like why you're able to manipulate shadows much the same way I can, except your technique seems… different. Maybe you're not manipulating the shadows so much as you are bending the light to use the shadow to your advantage."

She pondered that for a second, staring at the door that stood across from them. "I guess, maybe. I don't know. That's not something I've ever really contemplated."

"Did you ever really contemplate what you can do, though?"

"Yes, but not in that way. In the 'why can I do this' way, though? Yes. Why do you want to help me?" She asked, shrugging.

"Truthfully?"

"Obviously."

"My father, last night…He didn't even realize he'd killed your parents. When I brought it up, he deflected the blame onto Maddox and acted like it was nothing." He paused. "Then he teased me about not realizing what you are and asked me how I wanted to use you."

"How you want to use me?" Ice filled her voice. "Use me?"

"I know, it's callous and misogynistic. I didn't answer him. I didn't have an answer." He reached for her hand and squeezed it gently when she didn't pull away. "I don't think using someone for their abilities is the right thing to do, and I don't want to be involved in whatever scheme he's working on."

"You don't?"

"No, I don't. I knew he wasn't a great person, but…he had your family murdered for gods know what reason. He's killed others. I always suspected, but I could never prove anything. To have it confirmed…" he trailed off. "I don't want to be a part of this."

Sayah caught his eye and he quickly looked away, focusing on his hands. He began picking at a cuticle, pretending to be unaffected by his admission.

"If you don't want to be part of this, what are you going to do?" she asked, studying him.

"I'm going to work against him and try to stop whatever plot he has in the works."

She stood up, stretching her arms above her head. Her back arched, accentuating her uncorseted waist. Kage stared at her out of the corner of his eye.

Mmm, he thought. *She really is stunning.*

She stretched again, going up onto her toes, then came back down onto flat feet and looked at him. He smiled at her, then returned to picking at his cuticle, pretending that he hadn't been admiring her as she stretched.

"So," he said casually, "what do you want to do?"

"I'm not sure what you mean," Sayah said. "You kidnapped me, so none of this has really been about what I want, has it? It doesn't seem like the decision is up to me."

"No, but what happens from here is up to you. Do you want to stay, or do you want me to take you back to The

Rusty Pig?" He kept his face free of emotion, but his mind was reeling at the idea of her leaving.

"Are those the two options? Stay here in the house of my parents' murderer or leave to go back to a life on the streets?"

"The way I see it is this: you can stay here with me and work against my father from within his organization, or I can take you back to The Rusty Pig and go up against my father on my own."

"There's another option you haven't considered. Take me back to The Rusty Pig…but come with me," she said. "We can hide out there and try to learn more about what I can do, then we work against your father." Surprised shock showed on her face at the words that had come out of her mouth. "I mean—"

"You want me to come to a tavern with you." Kage's eyebrows shot up toward his hairline, his eyes dancing with amusement.

"You want to help me. I want to let Bess know that I'm okay. And I want to have some of her beef pie." She smiled.

"Beef pie?" he asked. "I do love beef pie."

"Is that a yes?"

"Well, it's not a no."

She smirked at him. "Let's get going, then."

CHAPTER TWELVE

K age led Sayah through the empty hallway outside his room and down the servants' stairs at the back of the house.

"I used to sneak out this way when I was younger," he said conversationally as they walked through the empty corridors. "Father hasn't employed servants in years, and the brothel's patrons aren't allowed in the personal quarters. Nobody uses these stairs anymore."

Sayah stayed quiet, focused, as they reached the ground floor and walked through the door at the back of the house. Kage led her down the short brick stairs and into the familiar alley. As they walked in the direction of The Rusty Pig, she tossed a glance back over her shoulder at the house.

"Where did it go?" she asked, shocked to see nothing but a blank brick wall behind them.

"Father has it cloaked and disguised. From the alley, it appears to be a large brick wall and old stairs that lead to nothing. From the street, it appears to be a discrete, well-appointed brothel, and from the other alley, a seedier brothel that caters to sailors, soldiers, and the working class."

Sayah nodded mutely. They passed through the alley, dodging around refuse and discarded crates and barrels, then strode out into the street. Throngs of roughly dressed people walked along the street, and the market stalls were full of merchandise.

"But wait," she said suddenly. "If it's cloaked, how did I see it the night—"

"The shadows dissipate for a few moments whenever someone enters through that door. Because Reisu and I stood in the doorway and spoke before I crossed the threshold, the spell couldn't take effect again."

"I see," Sayah mumbled, her thoughts churning.

"Oranges here, get your oranges here," cried one barker outside a fruit stall. "Fresh oranges, just arrived from Astraea on the merchant ships."

Sayah glanced in the direction of the barker, catching sight of the piles of oranges in the cart's baskets. She stopped, staring at the fruit.

"Sayah," Kage said. "What are you doing? We need to go."

"I just—I don't know. Astraea and oranges seem so familiar to me. Papa traveled often on the ships he helped design and build, and the oranges… I think he brought them back for us once."

"Would you like one?" he asked, pulling a small coin pouch out of his boot.

She opened her mouth to refuse, but he was already in the stall, grabbing a small basket of oranges and purchasing them. The merchant bundled them in cloth and handed them to Kage, who bowed slightly as he left. He handed her one and began to walk again.

"Thank you," she said quietly.

"You're welcome. Now, who is Bess?"

"A friend. I came across her one night in the alley behind the Pig, fending off a pair of men. She had been taking scraps out for the compost bin when they jumped her. I saved her, and she gave me food. Ever since, I've been able to find a hot meal at the tavern, and she often hid me in the stables or pump house so that I had a dry place to stay."

Kage's jaw dropped before he could stop it. "You saved her? How?"

"I cloaked myself in the shadows and ran forward, knocking the men out of the way. I grabbed her and wrapped her in the shadows with me and we ran back into the kitchens," Sayah explained. "She was terrified, but when she saw that I was a woman, she calmed down and told me what happened."

"You're a marvel," Kage said. "Truly."

"I'm not a marvel, Kage," Sayah said. "I'm just someone who couldn't stand by and watch a woman get hurt when I could do something to stop it."

"That makes you a marvel."

Sayah rolled her eyes. "Anyway, Bess feeds me when she can, and she's the cook at The Rusty Pig, so the food is always great."

They walked the rest of the way to the tavern in companionable silence. As they arrived, Sayah led Kage around to the back of the building and up the stairs to the kitchens.

"Bess?" She called out as she opened the door.

"Sayah," Bess said. "Thank gods you're here. Where have you been? You've been gone for days."

"Remember the boy I told you about, the one with my abilities?"

"Of course I remember, you went looking for him and then disappeared."

"He found me, and he sort of kidnapped me," Sayah said.

"But you can't be mad at him, because it turned out to be a good thing."

"He did what?" Bess's eyes flashed. "I can absolutely be mad at him if I want to," she said, her cheeks ruddy with temper. "If I ever lay my eyes on him—"

"I suppose I should hide outside?" Kage asked Sayah.

"He didn't harm me in any way, Bess," Sayah said, "so I would prefer that you not harm him. But he did help me figure out what happened to my parents, who did it, and we have a theory about why I have the ability to manipulate shadows and where it came from."

"I reserve the right to stab him if he pisses me off," Bess said. "But I guess he can come in."

"Thank you." Sayah gathered her friend close for a hug.

"I hope you won't stab me," Kage said. "Sayah hasn't stopped talking about your beef pie, and I desperately want to try it."

"Lucky for you, it's Sayah's favorite, so I always have one made. Since she says I can't cause you bodily harm, I suppose I'll have to let you eat." Bess got out three plates and sets of utensils, setting them on the table, then grabbed the pie from the counter and cut them each a generous slice. "Sit, eat."

Kage obliged, pulling out chairs for Sayah and Besa before he settled himself. Bess harrumphed to herself but allowed him to seat her. Sayah settled into her seat, and Kage smiled at her as he shifted in his chair. His knee brushed against Sayah's skirts and he flushed slightly. Her nearness threw him slightly off balance; he couldn't put a finger on why, but it bothered him. He tucked into the pie that Bess put in front of him, scooping a heaping spoonful into his mouth.

"Oh gods," he said after swallowing the buttery crust and

rich beef gravy. "This is delicious. More than delicious—it's downright heavenly."

Sayah laughed. "I told you," she said. "Bess makes the best beef pie."

"I don't know about the best," Bess said, "but it's an old family recipe."

"Is that tarragon?" Kage asked, licking the last drops of gravy from his spoon. He looked longingly at the remaining pie that sat on the counter across from them.

Bess smirked at him. "I don't give away family recipes."

"Oh."

"Why don't you go ahead and tell me about kidnapping Sayah and what you discovered," she said, her eyes narrowed. "And while you do that, I'll bring the rest of that pie over. If I like what I hear, maybe I'll allow you another slice."

"What do you want to know?" Kage asked, salivating at the thought of more pie.

"Everything. For starters, how did you find her?" Bess asked, reaching out to take Sayah's hand. "Was she in danger?"

"With me? No, absolutely not. With the rest of the world? No idea. I can't speak for them," Kage responded. "As for how I found her, it's a pretty convoluted story. Ultimately, I found her much the same way she had hoped to find me: by looking for anomalies in the shadows. I had seen her in the alley that night, hidden, and distracted the men who were after her so that she could get away. After I lost track of her myself, I returned home and asked Father about her."

"Father?"

"Yes. My father is Dal'gon, the shadow demon. Until I saw Sayah, the only people we know of that could manipulate the shadows were directly related to him."

"Your father," Bess said, "is a what?"

"He's the shadow demon. His sons are the only ones who can manipulate shadow, or so we thought. When I told him about Sayah, he charged me with kidnapping her and bringing her to him."

"He did?" Sayah looked shocked.

"Yes, that's why I was looking for you. That and my own curiosity. When he confirmed that you weren't one of his disciples, as he calls us, I wanted to know what you were."

"Okay, so your father made you look for her. Then what?" Bess tried to keep her face neutral, but her furrowed brow and the color in her cheeks belied her upset.

"I caught a glimpse of her one afternoon and followed her through the market, then into the theater district. When she entered the library at the Lyceum, I followed her and waited until she was alone and distracted."

"Ironically, I was reading a book about his father when he revealed himself to me," Sayah cut in. "He didn't admit to that until later on, though."

"Interesting."

"I took her into the shadow realm and then on to my father's house, as I was instructed. She told me about her parents and the discovery of her powers, and then my father unintentionally gave us another piece of the puzzle," Kage said, his face serious. "Sayah doesn't have demon blood. She is descended from angels."

"What?" Bess shouted. She shook her head. "You're pulling my leg, and I don't take kindly to that."

"No, we don't think Dal'gon is wrong about this," Sayah said. "I remembered more about the day my parents were murdered, about my mother. She was chanting in a language I didn't know, and she glowed, Bess. Glowed like the light of a thousand candles shone from inside her skin."

"And the man who killed her parents...he used shadows to do it. He is my oldest brother, Maddox. My father's heir apparent."

"Get out," Bess said, "before I have the bruiser out front toss you out himself."

"No, Bess." Sayah steeled her voice and gripped her friend's hand. "Kage had nothing to do with it. He would have been a child at the time, not much older than I was, if I'm not mistaken." She looked to Kage, who nodded affirmatively. "When he found out and confirmed it with his father... that's why he's here with me."

"That is a lot to process," Bess said. "I can't even—"

"I know." Kage looked at Sayah and gave her a small smile, gently bumping his knee into hers. "But we both made it here alive, and now we get to enjoy this fantastic beef pie."

Sayah smiled back shyly. Bess studied the two of them, giving Kage a very discerning look. Sighing, she cut another portion of the pie and slid it onto his plate.

"What do you plan to do next?" Bess asked.

"We're going to figure out why my father targeted Sayah's family, and then we're going to find a way to defeat him," Kage said, trying to keep pie crumbs from falling out of his mouth as he spoke.

"And we're going to figure out exactly where my powers come from," Sayah added. "We're going to find out why I can manipulate shadows and why my mother...was what she was. Whatever she was."

Bess leaned back in her chair and set down her spoon. "How can I help?"

Kage and Sayah exchanged a glance.

Sayah took a deep breath. "Here's what I was thinking..."

CHAPTER THIRTEEN

The Rusty Pig boasted several single occupancy rooms and one two bedroom suite of rooms with a sitting area and private dining room. After speaking with Bess for some time, going over the plan and their needs in detail, Kage paid the owner handsomely for access to the suite until they no longer needed it. As Bess showed them to the suite, she sent for a large copper tub to be brought into the room so Sayah could have a bath. Kage walked through the rooms, securely weaving shadows around each window and door to prevent eavesdropping.

The kitchen boy and one of the barkeeps carried up the massive tub, placing it before the fireplace in Sayah's room. The kitchen boy returned several times with pails of hot water, filling the tub nearly to the top. He poured a small vial into the tub before bowing and leaving the room. Steam rose from the surface of the water, the scent of lavender and rosemary filling the air from the oil that floated within. Bess entered the room carrying a pile of thick towels and a cake of soap, setting them on a small table beside the tub.

"Thank you," Sayah said, accepting Bess's hand to stand beside the tub. She began to unlace the stays at her shoulders and shed the top layer of her skirts. "I can't remember the last time I had a real bath in hot water with soap."

"I'm glad that you'll get one now," Bess said. "That gentleman you've met, he seems determined to protect you."

"I think he was rather ambivalent at first," Sayah said. "But after he discovered what his father and brother had done... He feels obligated to help me find the truth."

"Obligation wouldn't make him look at you the way he does," Bess said knowingly. "Be careful, Sayah."

"I will, Bess. You know that I won't let him do anything to hurt me." She struggled with a knot in the laces at the back of her underdress.

"It's your heart I'm worried about, not your body. You've had so little love in your life," Bess said emphatically as she began to pick out the knot. "Don't go falling in love with him without so much as a *by your leave*, you hear me?"

"Yes, I hear you. I won't. I don't want love. I want to know why I can do these things and why Dal'gon killed my parents." Sayah let Bess finish unlacing her underdress, then shrugged out of the heavy fabric, letting it look at her feet. She stepped from the puddle of fabric hissed out a breath as Bess helped her climb into the tub, the hot water heating her skin to a pleasant shade of pink.

"Here," Bess said as Sayah sank into the water up to her shoulders. "Let me wash your hair."

Sayah nodded and leaned back, letting the water drench her hair. As Bess massaged her scalp and worked the soap through the long, tangled strands of hair, she let her mind wander back to the beforetimes. The knots in her neck and shoulders released at the gentle pressure of Bess's fingers, and she slipped gently into a state of relaxation. The memories were hazy, at best.

But perhaps, if I focus, I can remember something else, she thought, letting herself drift amidst the comfort of the warm water and gentle massage.

She sat in the tub, splashing as her mama knelt beside her and soaped her hair with a bar of lemon scented soap.

"There, there, little fish, not much longer now. Once we rinse, you can swim away," Mama said with laughter in her voice as Sayah kicked her feet and splashed water out of the tub.

"Mama, I'm not a fish," Sayah said, giggling and squirming. "I'm a little girl."

"Oh, I know, poppet." Mama's eyes glowed a little brighter as she smiled at Sayah and brushed a soapy strand of hair back over her shoulder. "Now, let's rinse your hair so you can go play. When we're done, do you want to play with your dolls or your sailboats?"

Sayah smiled playfully and puffed her cheeks full of air, ducking under the water and pretending to be a dolphin like the ones she saw from Papa's ship. When she popped up above the surface, Mama jumped, pretending to be surprised.

"Mama, maybe I am a fish," she said excitedly.

"Of course you are, poppet," Mama said before mumbling under her breath. "Benedicite peuri. Custodire eam."

"What does that mean, Mama?"

"It's just a prayer, my love. One I say every day."

"But why?"

"Because words and intentions have power, more than most people realize. So I pray and hope that everything will be okay." Mama tucked a strand of wet hair behind Sayah's

ear and leaned in to kiss her forehead. "You are my miracle,
Sayah. Papa and I will protect you with everything we have
in us."

Sayah drifted back to the present, feeling Bess's hands,
strong from years of kneading bread dough, massaging her
scalp and gently working out the knots in her hair.

"Do you think she knew?" Sayah asked.

"Who? Knew what?" Bess looked confused.

"My mother," Sayah said. "Do you think Mama knew I
was special?"

"I'm sure she did," Kage said, opening the door and
popping his head around it. "I wasn't eavesdropping, just
coming to tell you that there is a small spread of bread and
cheese in the sitting room, and a pot of tea, if you're so
inclined."

"We can discuss more once I'm done?" Sayah asked. "I'd
like to hear Bess's opinions now."

"Of course," he said. "I'll leave you to finish." He ducked
back through the door and closed it behind him.

"I think she would have known you had some form of
ability. From what you described earlier, she was something
more than human herself, so she would have recognized signs
in you, probably before you even knew," Bess said. "Could
you lean back so I can rinse your hair? I think I've gotten all
the tangles out."

Sayah leaned back obediently, letting Bess work her
fingers through the long strands, rinsing the soap and
ensuring all of the tangles and knots were free. "I can't help
but wonder," she said, "if Mama knew that I could manipulate shadows this way. I wish there was a way for me to find
out what she knew."

"I wish there was, too. Unfortunately, we can't go back in
time or speak with the dead."

"Maybe I'll remember something, or we'll learn something now that Kage is helping me."

"Maybe," Bess said. "You're all rinsed. Let's get you dried off and dressed so you can have tea with the dark prince waiting out in the sitting room."

"Don't call him that, Bess! That's ridiculous. He's not a prince."

"Dark lordling, then?"

"Oh stop," Sayah said, giggling. She stood in the tub, the sluice of water running down her delicate curves.

Bess handed her a towel and laid another on the ground next to the tub, then helped Sayah step out of the tub. While Sayah dried off her body, Bess focused on her hair, drying it and then working a wooden comb through the thick strands to finish off the last of the tangles and knots.

Kage paced the floor in the sitting room, waiting for Sayah to get out of her bath.

"Gods, does it always take women so bloody long to bathe?" he muttered to himself. "A body could starve waiting for a woman to finish with her hair."

The door creaked behind him and he sat down quickly, crossing one foot onto his knee and leaning back into the cushions of the leather wing chair beside the fireplace. Sayah walked through the door, wrapped in a dressing gown with a delicate floral pattern. Her long, dark curls were damp and hung down her back to her waist.

"Hi," Sayah said.

"Hi," Kage said, standing from the chair. "You look refreshed." He grasped her hand and led her to the chair across from his, seating her beside the fire.

"Thanks. It was nice to get a hot bath." She settled back into the cushions of the chair and reached for the teapot on the small table beside them. "Tea?"

"Yes, I would love some," he said.

She poured them each a cup, dropping a sugar cube and a splash of milk into her own.

"Just lemon, please."

She squeezed a lemon wedge into his tea and handed him the cup and saucer, her hands shaking slightly, then grabbed a small chunk of Brie from the platter.

"Mmm," she said as she chewed on the soft, ripe cheese. "This is delicious."

Kage smiled and took a slice of dark wheat bread from the platter, smearing it with rich, creamy butter. He took a bite and smiled wider. "This is amazing," he said. "Bess made this, too?"

"Yes, she does all the baking," Sayah said. "She's brilliant."

"She really is. This is the best bread I've ever had."

"The demon's chef must bake subpar bread, then," Bess said as she popped her head in. "Sayah, do you want to go through my dresses to see if any of the others suit you?"

"That won't be necessary," Kage said. "I thought I could take her to the seamstress and milliner tomorrow to outfit her."

"You thought you would do what?" Sayah asked, color rising in her cheeks. "You thought you would do…what?" She stressed the last word heavily, her eyes narrowed into a tense glare.

Kage held his hands up. "I thought I would take you to pick out some clothes and a hat or two. Since you only have the two dresses. Or I thought you only—"

"Why is that any of your business?" Sayah looked over her shoulder to where Bess stood in the doorway. "Why should I take charity from the likes of you? So you can turn me into your little pity project? Bess, can you believe—"

"Don't look at me," Bess said. "I think it's nice."

"Wh—" Sayah stopped, shaking her head. "Why do you want to take me shopping?" she asked Kage.

"Because," Kage said, "I want to. You would have grown up in safety with people who loved you if it wasn't for my family."

"See? Exactly. You don't owe me anything," Sayah said. "You didn't do—"

"I owe you so much more than you know," Kage said. "If I hadn't seen you that night, where would I be? What would Father have me doing? I don't want to think about it."

Sayah stared at him, her mouth open in shock. Bess came the rest of the way into the room and shut the door. She laid a hand on Sayah's shoulder.

"Kage," Bess said, squeezing Sayah's shoulder gently. "I'm sure you realize that Sayah hasn't had an easy life since she lost her parents. But she wasn't—"

"She wasn't alone the whole time. I know. She told me about meeting you."

"She did?"

"Yes," Sayah said. "You cared for me when I had nobody else, and we talked about my life after I lost Mama and Papa." She reached a hand up and grasped Bess's hand. "I couldn't have survived without you."

"You could have, and you did for many years," Bess said. "But I'm glad we found each other."

"Sayah," Kage said, his voice quiet. "Would you be willing to let me take you shopping?"

"I suppose," she said. "But only if you stop this talk about owing me. You owe me nothing."

"Okay," Kage said.

Sayah smiled. "I do like the idea of a fancy hat."

Behind them, shadows swirled just outside the leaded glass windows, searching for an opening.

CHAPTER FOURTEEN

ayah woke with the first light of dawn as it shone in
through the delicate curtains that hung across the east
facing windows. The warm colors of the sunrise
danced across her eyelids, slowly bringing her back to
consciousness. A small smile drifted across her face as she
rolled onto her back and stretched her arms up toward the
flocked velvet headboard. She hummed quietly to herself,
pulling the thick quilt and sheet more tightly around her
shoulders and reveling in the soft mattress and warmth from
the blanket cocoon surrounding her.

She sighed. *I don't ever want to leave this bed,* she
thought. *I just want to lay here in the warmth and remember
what it feels like to be safe.* A soft knock on the door startled
her.

"Bess?" she asked.

"Not quite." Kage said as he walked into the room, dark
circles ringing his eyes. He sat down on the chair beside the
fireplace and put his feet up on the small dressing table. His
large leather boots shone from polish, but his haggard face

belied a sleepless night. Sayah sat up, pulling the covers over her chest.

"You look like hell," Sayah said.

"Thanks. You sure know how to make a man feel good about himself. I couldn't sleep," Kage said. "The sunrise is beautiful, though."

"It is. The warmth of the light woke me this morning."

"Do you always wake with the dawn?" Kage asked.

"For as long as I can remember. I've always loved the way the light paints the sky in pastels."

"It is a special kind of beauty." Kage looked at Sayah, studying the graceful lines of her face and the riotous tumble of curls down her back. "Just like you."

"Thanks, I think." Sayah brushed an errant curl back behind her ear and stretched forward, arching her back like a cat.

"Will you need any help getting dressed?" Kage asked.

"Just with lacing up my dress," Sayah said. "Unless you think I should wear a corset."

"Can't we have you fitted for one of those things while we're there?"

"I have no idea." The delicate strap of her borrowed chemise slid off her shoulder and she absentmindedly dragged it back into place. "I've never been to a modiste before."

"It's not like you need one," Kage said, raking his fingers through his hair. "Your waist is—"

"Don't." Sayah said. "Don't even start. You sound like an idiot spouting poetry."

"Oh. Okay." A sheepish look crossed his face at her reprimand.

A businesslike knock at the door interrupted them, followed by the creaking of hinges.

"Sayah?" Bess called out. "I brought breakfast up. Do you want me to lace up your dress?"

"That would be nice. Thanks so much, Bess."

"Out." Bess pointed Kage out the bedroom door. "You can wait for us in the sitting room."

Kage nodded and left the room, closing the door behind him.

Bess smirked at Sayah. "In your bedroom?" she asked.

"It's not like I invited him," Sayah said. "He just came in as I was waking up. The sunrise was beautiful." She stood and crossed to where Bess readied the dress and petticoats, grasping her friend's hand quickly. "Thank you. For everything."

"You're welcome." Bess held out the petticoats for Sayah to step into and secured them around her waist. "In your bedroom," she muttered.

"Oh, stop," Sayah said. "Nothing happened."

"Yet." Bess giggled, and the two of them fell into each other's arms, laughing hysterically.

Kage sat at the small breakfast table in the sitting room, listening to the joyous sound of female laughter coming from Sayah's bedroom. *I wonder what's so amusing,* he thought with a small smile. He spooned clotted cream onto a warm scone flecked with sanding sugar and delicate flecks of orange zest. The first bite of the flaky pastry crumbled pleasantly under the pressure of his teeth and the coolness of the clotted cream chilled his tongue as the orange zest teased his senses. Flames danced in the fireplace beside him, warming the air and casting flickering shadows around the room. He relaxed, listening to the peals of laughter from Sayah's room as he chewed thoughtfully on the scone.

"Delicious," he said. "Bess really is a genius."

A hissing noise came from the corner of the room, shadows flickering in the light of the flames. Kage's head snapped up, jolted from his thoughts as he recognized the all too familiar scent of brimstone in the fire.

"You never were good about double-checking your protections after a good night's sleep," a deep voice said from within the shadows. "It'll be the death of you one day. So this is where you've been hiding."

"I haven't been hiding, per se," Kage said, affecting the devil may care bravado he was known for amongst his siblings. "Hello, big brother. To what do I owe the pleasure?"

"Father is quite irritated with you for stealing his prize away." Maddox released the shadows that surrounded him, stepping into the room fully. The soft light from the windows gleamed off his bald pate. "Where is the girl?"

"Close," Kage said.

"Bring her back."

"Not gonna happen." Kage smirked. "I have plans for her."

"If you don't bring her back, he will come for her. You know that."

"Let him come."

"Fine. It's your funeral." Maddox stared at Kage in derision before stepping back into the shadows and twisting them. "Don't expect me to save you when he comes for your head." He disappeared without another word. Kage leaned back in his chair and took a deep breath, steadying himself.

How did he find us? And how did I never realize what a prick he is? he wondered. *And Father... Gods, he's even worse.* He sat, ruminating on his family and their disrepute, solemnly finishing his scone. As he lifted the teapot to pour himself a cup, Sayah's door opened and she and Bess walked into the sitting room.

Sayah's eyes lit up at the sight of the scones and fruit laid out before him. "Oh, scones," she exclaimed. "My favorite." She strode to the table and sat down, grabbing one from the platter and taking a massive bite.

"Try it with the clotted cream," Kage said, handing her the dish. "It's delicious."

Sayah took the dish from him and put a dollop of the cream onto the scone. Bess opened and secured the curtains, filling the room with bright morning sunlight and eradicating the few shadows that remained.

"Mmm," she said. "Ish ith tho good."

"What?" Bess asked, laughter in her tone.

Sayah swallowed, smiling sheepishly. "This is so good," she said.

Kage grinned at them. "Bess, did you make these, too?"

"Of course."

"They're wonderful."

"Thank you." She blushed slightly before straightening her back and screwing a frown onto her face. "Compliments won't make me like you any more, though. I'll consider changing my opinion of you when you keep my Sayah safe from that demon of a father you have."

"Sayah, do you think you'll be ready to go shopping after breakfast?" Kage asked as he dropped a few grapes and a slice of cantaloupe onto his plate.

"Yes, I'm ready now. Do you want to leave?"

"Only if you eat more than that one scone." He heaped fruit onto her plate.

She threw a grape at him, giggling as it bounced off of his plate and careened into his forehead. Bess snuck out of the room while they laughed. Kage threw the grape back at Sayah and she dodged, smacking her head into the table as she ducked to avoid it.

"Oh gods," Kage said as he leapt from his chair and went to her. He carefully cradled her face in his hands and looked at the small red mark that marred her forehead. "Are you okay?"

"I'm fine, I swear. Other than humiliation, that is." She blushed as he continued to study her face, gently probing her forehead with the tips of his fingers. "I'm okay, really."

He continued touching her forehead, softly stroking the delicate skin with his fingers to soothe the painful mark that remained where she had connected with the table. Her lips parted slightly, revealing the moist, delicate skin of the inside of her lip. She caught her lower lip between her teeth, pulling the soft, rosy skin taut. His heart pounded, and she watched as his pupils dilated, the fire in their depths igniting.

She is so beautiful, he thought as he stared at her mouth. *I could just...* He trailed a finger down her cheek and gently stroked it across her full lower lip, feeling the softness of her skin.

"Ahem," Bess interrupted as she entered the room. "It seems you've forgotten that you have plans this morning. Luckily, I haven't. Kage, please go see to procuring a carriage for your outing. I will see to Sayah's forehead and help her as tidy up so that she's ready when you are done."

Kage stood, gently taking Sayah's hand and helping her to her feet. "I'll be right back," he said softly, staring into her azure eyes.

"I'll be here," she said, swaying slightly.

He headed down the stairs and out the front of The Rusty Pig. As the sound of his boots faded, Bess turned to Sayah, her shoulders shaking with mirth.

"Oh gods, the way he looks at you. I told you," she said. "I knew it."

"Stop," Sayah said. "But really, though…the way he touched my lip—I was sure he was going to kiss me before you came back in."

Bess just smiled.

CHAPTER FIFTEEN

K age walked back into the tavern's taproom after procuring a carriage. The fire in the hearth heated the room and the smell of yeasty beer and bread permeated the air. He took a deep breath, admiring the homey scent. A creak on the stairs commanded his attention, and he looked up as Sayah descended. She held herself like royalty, with perfect posture and a slightly arrogant lift to her chin. Though the deep sapphire dress was borrowed, the color was perfect for her, adding depth to her azure eyes and making her dark hair appear even more lustrous. Her curls were twisted and pinned into some sort of twist, the dangling strands brushing against her neck.

"You look fantastic," Kage said, mesmerized.

"Thank you." Sayah appraised his appearance, looking him up and down. "You look very nice, too."

Suddenly nervous, Kage wiped his palms on his tan breeches and reached out to take Sayah's hand. "We should get going."

Sayah didn't argue, letting him lead her out the door and onto the street. He handed her up into the carriage and climbed in behind her. As Bess came to the front door of the tavern, Sayah leaned from the carriage window and waved to her jauntily.

Kage gave a signal to the driver and the carriage moved forward, the horses whinnying in response to the click of the reins. He leaned against the velvet squabs and steepled his fingers, watching Sayah as she pushed the curtain aside once more and stared out the window as they rolled through the streets to the merchant district. A smile lit her face at the light breeze coming through the window.

"Ship's Haven looks so different from the window of a carriage," Sayah said, awe in her voice.

"It's the same city, but the movement of the carriage blurs the harsh reality a bit," Kage replied. "It hides some of the more questionable aspects. Are you warm enough?"

Sayah looked at him, confused. "Why wouldn't I be warm enough?"

"It's a little cool out," Kage said. "There are lap blankets, if you would like one."

"I'm fine, thank you."

Kage nodded. He closed his eyes and leaned back against the velvet again. They hit a large bump that jostled them, throwing Sayah onto his lap. He caught her before she slid off of him onto the floor, pulling her closer to him and bracing his hands on her waist. Her forehead smacked into the seat behind him and she erupted into a fit of giggles.

"Hi," she said, a dazed look on her face as she laughed.

"Hi." Kage's pupils dilated as he stared at her grinning mouth. Startling them both, he pulled her against his chest and lowered his mouth to hers, plundering her soft lips. He grasped her waist tighter, shifting her body closer to him.

A quiet moan left her throat as he moved his hands over her uncorseted waist and caressed her back. He slid his tongue against the opening of her mouth, parting her lips gently before slipping inside.

"Oh!" Sayah jumped, shocked, and pulled away. She touched her lips, her eyes slightly dazed, and then stared at him. Confusion and lust filled her eyes, making their azure depths even more vibrant.

A low groan escaped Kage's throat as she hopped over to the other side of the carriage. She leaned closer, bridging the gap between them, and took his hand in both of hers. She studied his long fingers and broad palms, running her fingertips over the ridges and valleys that marked his individuality. With his other hand, Kage gently grasped her chin and lifted her eyes to his.

"If you keep touching me like that, I'm going to kiss you again," he said.

"Is that a threat?" She seemed incredulous at the thought. Her teeth bit into one side of her lower lip as she continued to clasp his hand between her own.

"No. It's a promise." He smiled at her, admiring the swollen lips and blush on her cheeks from their kiss.

She bristled at his words, fiery light filling her eyes. "I hope you like to break promises," she said, "because I have no intention of allowing you to kiss me again after that."

"Oh, Sayah. Not only will I kiss you again… you'll ask me to kiss you."

She opened her mouth to speak, but quickly shut it again when she couldn't find the words to adequately express her frustration with his ridiculous assertions. She tilted to the side as they rounded a corner to the left, grasping the seat to keep from falling into Kage's lap again. As they passed another city block, the carriage slowed and came to a stop. Sayah studied the gray stone facade of the modiste's shop, carved with roses and fleur de lis. A large plate glass window stood at the front, showcasing a mannequin wearing a stunning black dress that shimmered in silk and metallic embroidery.

"This is the place?" she asked.

"Yes."

"Madame Archambault," Sayah read. "French?"

"*Mais oui, ma chérie,*" Kage replied. "The French are always at the forefront of style."

A small smile tweaked the corners of her mouth at his abysmal French accent. "The dress in the window is lovely." As the carriage door swung open, she slid over and grasped the driver's hand, allowing him to hand her down from the plush interior.

Kage hopped out and opened the door to the modiste's shop, holding it open for Sayah. Madame Archambault swept into the room at the sound of the chimes, her skirts swirling around her legs. The delicate rustle of petticoats against silk seemed to echo in the pristine silence of the room.

"Welcome, welcome," she said. "How can I help you?"

Kage gestured at Sayah, a smile on his face. "The lady requires some new gowns, undergarments… the whole kit."

"Ah, yes, *monsieur*. We shall find your lady some beautiful things. Does my lady have colors she particularly likes?" Madam Archambault looked at Sayah, evaluating her choice of clothing and the fit. "This was made for someone else, was it not?"

"Yes," Sayah said. "It was loaned to me by a friend because I did not have an appropriate dress."

"Ah, *oui*. And no corset, either? But such a tiny waist. Come with me, my darling, and we shall begin." Madame Archambault grasped Sayah's hand in hers and led her to a private dressing area toward the back of the store. "Now tell me, *ma belle,* what is your favorite color?"

"I've always liked green," Sayah said.

Kage smiled as he seated himself in one of the chairs in the main area of the shop. The delicately carved mahogany legs and tufted rolled arms appeared comfortable, but he felt grossly oversized for the feminine chair and shifted uncomfortably in his seat. A plethora of fabric bolts lined shelves on the wall, arranged in a colorful rainbow of patterns and fabrics. A forest green muslin with tiny vines and leaves in sage green stood out to him, and he made a mental note to show it to Sayah once she came back. He attempted to leaned back in the chair and nearly tipped over. Sighing, he stood and wandered to the window, tapping his fingers against his thigh and watching the crowd pass by.

Madame Archambault was ruthlessly efficient with her tape measure and pins, whipping around Sayah as she worked. "Amelie, pay attention. 34 inch hips, 25 inch waist," she snapped to her assistant, who scrawled notes into her ledger. "34 and a half inch bust. Quite the figure, *ma belle*, and without a corset to cinch you in. Let's get you into some proper undergarments so that we can get you fitted into something that suits you."

"Okay," Sayah said.

She turned as Madame Archambault gestured to her. Her thin chemise ended at the tops of her thighs, leaving the rest of her bare. She carefully stepped into the bloomers Madame held out for her, suddenly aware of her nudity as the undergarments covered her delicate skin. The assistant, a small, mousy girl with pale ivory skin and eyes the color of late winter ice, fitted a boned corset to Sayah's torso and began lacing her into a it, nipping in her waist and ending just below her breasts, thrusting them upward. As she turned to face the mirror, she gasped.

"I know," Madame Archambault said, gently laying a hand on her lower back. "You are beautiful."

"And we haven't even dressed you yet," the assistant said, her eyes filled with excitement.

"Come, Sayah." Madame Archambault led her from the room.

Kage jumped as they entered, and Madame Archambault laughed boisterously. "Young man, no need to be startled. Did you see anything you like while you waited?"

Kage blushed, staring at Sayah as a flush of red rushed toward his hairline. "Um, I, ah…" he stuttered.

Sayah's shoulders shook with suppressed laughter. "You what?"

"I thought this would be nice," he said, gesturing toward the forest green muslin with a small frown on his face. "Green is lovely on you."

Madame Archambault pulled the bolt of fabric from the shelf and unwound several yards, draping them across Sayah's shoulders and chest. "Oh yes, *monsieur*, a wonderful choice. What style does my lady prefer?"

"What style?" Sayah looked perplexed.

"Yes, *mademoiselle*, what style. The bustle, the petticoats, the hoop skirt… what do you prefer?"

Sayah froze, and Kage stepped forward to grasp her arm. He led her across the room to the well appointed mannequins along the right of the shop.

"This," he said, pointing toward a dress featuring a large rear end, "is a bustle."

"Oh, absolutely not. That's absurd."

"I think just petticoats," Kage said. "And a pair of

breeches and a waistcoat so that she can move freely when
she needs to."

"But *monsieur–*"

"No buts. There will be times she will need to be able to
move around without the restriction of skirts and petticoats."
Kage smiled. "And I'll have the added benefit of enjoying the
sight of her wearing them."

Sayah smacked his arm. A sudden movement in the
corner caught her eye, but nothing was there when she turned
her head fully to look. On the other side of the shop, a brilliant silk the color of shadows in a forest caught her eye. Not
quite gray but not quite green, the color of the silk shimmered
and shifted as the light caught it. "Oh," she said, placing her
hand over her heart. "That is lovely."

"Mademoiselle has excellent taste," Madame Archambault said. "The dupioni silk is extremely beautiful and
unique. Best used for nightclothes or a ball gown."

"I don't believe we have need of a ball gown, but Sayah
could definitely use some nightclothes. Maybe a corset of the
material, as well?"

"Yes, Monsieur, we can do that." Madame Archambault
gestured to her assistant. "Amelie, fetch that bolt of cloth and
set it aside."

"We will also need the muslin in a day dress, and this gray—"

"Do you think I could choose my own clothing?" Sayah
asked. Color rose in her cheeks.

"The kitten has claws," Madame whispered to Amelie,
watching the confrontation unfold.

"Of course," Kage said. "Would it be acceptable to you if
I provide some input, as I'm the one paying for everything?"

"I'm not a doll for you to dress. But yes, I will entertain
your suggestions."

Kage walked to a bolt of gray fabric, a soft linen with a faint grid-like pattern. "This," he said.

"Oh, that is pretty. Can we see what else I like before we decide on anything else?"

"Sure."

She walked along the shelves, running her fingers across the bolts of fabric. Shimmering silks, lush velvets, sumptuous brocades, and delicately patterned muslins teased her senses as she touched them. Her breath caught in her throat at the sight of a dense velvet the color of twilight. "This one," she said, breathless.

"Definitely," Kage replied.

Amelie hurried to grab the fabric and add it to the others. "Mademoiselle," she said, "if I may suggest this brushed cotton, as well?" She pointed to a bolt of turquoise woven into an ivory and silver plaid. "This color, it would be perfect with your eyes."

"Oh, yes," Sayah gushed. "Yes, that's absolutely perfect!"

Kage smiled at the joy in her voice and nodded his agreement to the modiste.

"I believe we have something ready in this pattern," Madame Archambault said. "Amelie, please fetch the dress for us and we shall fit it for her."

CHAPTER SIXTEEN

Sayah twirled in a circle as they left the *modiste*, endlessly pleased with the flowing skirt and rustling petticoats. She adjusted the small straw hat's turquoise ribbons so that they flowed down alongside the curls that spilled from her twisted updo. Madame Archambault had managed to find a dainty pair of slippers that matched the turquoise of the dress perfectly, and Sayah's feet floated along the cobblestones in the first new shoes she had owned in gods' knew how many years.

Kage chuckled quietly as he watched her skip, swirling her skirts and grinning. "Where to now?" he asked.

Sayah stopped suddenly and whipped around, her skirts swirling around her ankles. "What do you mean?"

"Where do you want to go now?"

"I thought we were just going back to The Rusty Pig. You want to go somewhere else?" She looked perplexed.

"I like seeing you smile. If you would like to go into some other shops, we can absolutely do that," Kage said.

"You like seeing me smile?"

Kage blushed and looked away. "What if we go to the tea

shop a few streets down? Or we could get ice cream at the Italian shop over on Canal Street?"

"I've never had ice cream," Sayah said sheepishly, as though she was admitting that she had an extra toe or some other equally embarrassing ailment.

"What? No way. Then we are definitely getting ice cream." Kage's voice echoed with his excitement. "Let me tell the driver so we can go." He alerted their carriage driver and gestures toward their destination, then grabbed her hand and led her down the street toward the ice cream shop.

He likes seeing me smile, Sayah thought. Butterflies flitted around her stomach as she relived their kiss earlier. *I like seeing him smile, too. I might even have liked kissing him.*

She let him lead her through the mid-afternoon crowds along Canal Street, content to look around at the people and buildings that surrounded her. Everything shone a little bit brighter in the golden afternoon sunlight, and the gondoliers of the Canal District stood in the bows of their boats, shouting to one another as they steered their charges through the wide canals. She sighed quietly as she watched them navigate through the water, then stumbled as she bumped into a wide back, clad in rough brown fabric.

"Oy, watch where ya goin'," the man said, glaring at Sayah as she and Kage passed him.

"So sorry," Kage said. "Won't happen again." He grasped Sayah's hand tighter and picked up the pace, nearly jogging through the crowd. He dodged around a street cart full of cabbages and ducked into an alley that ran between two narrow buildings.

Sayah's vision blurred as she spun around in the alley, disoriented by the strange smell of pine and alcohol that surrounded them. She looked at Kage, who stood doubled over against the pale brick wall of the boarding house that blocked them from view, catching his breath.

"What was that about?" she asked, shaking her skirts free of the cabbage remnants that had spilled on her as they ran.

"The man you bumped into," Kage said, his breath coming in short pants. "I know him. He works for my father."

"He… oh." Sayah's face fell and she braced herself against the wall as the strength left her body. "Do you think…"

"If he doesn't know where we are yet, he will find out soon," Kage said, his face serious. "I won't lie to you, Sayah. He views you as a prize that he won. When I ran off with you, that was a double slight. I took something he feels entitled to, and he views that as a betrayal. But I also chose someone else over him."

"And nobody has ever done that before? Chosen to leave, or taken something from him?"

"No. Nobody. His disciples are all addicted to the power he gives them and the abilities they possess." Kage wiped his hand across his forehead. "The ability to manipulate shadow can corrupt, and Dal'gon has perfected ways to use the shadows to get what he wants out of his disciples."

"Wh-what does that mean for me?" Sayah stuttered, her voice soft despite the volume of the nearby crowd.

"He wants you," Kage said. "He views you as important to whatever scheme he's cooking up right now, and he won't stop until he has you back."

Sayah's face fell at the thought of being trapped by Dal'gon, and Kage took a step toward her. Down the alley, shadows swirled and twisted, coalescing into a solid shape for a split second before disappearing again. An otherworldly chuckle floated toward them from the shadows. Kage grabbed a hold of Sayah's arm and pulled her to him, twisting so that she was against the brick wall and shielded from danger by his body. A whip of shadow lashed out at them, striking Kage across the shoulders and wrapping around his arm. It yanked backward, trying to pull him off of Sayah, but he held his ground steadily and stayed in place, cradling her against his body with her cheek pressed against his chest. His heart pounded from the exertion as he used every ounce of power he had to build a shield around them to help him stand strong against the onslaught of shadow attacks that pummeled him. He felt Sayah's panic as it rose in her chest, sharp spikes of anxiety in her eyes. She began to glow softly and his eyes widened as she threw up a shield around them, a golden shell that surrounded them like a second skin. The balls of shadow and flame that penetrated Kage's shield hit Sayah's, falling harmless to the ground and extinguishing.

"This isn't over," Maddox's voice said through the shadows. "Father will have her, and you will be punished." A cloud of swirling shadow flew past them, kicking up dust and detritus from the alley as it blew through.

The shadows around them lessened, allowing light back into the area as Maddox disappeared.

Kage rested his forehead against the wall just above Sayah's head, desperate to steady himself so that he could get her out of the alley and back to their rooms. "I'm sorry, Sayah," he said. "This is all my fault."

"How is this your fault?" she asked.

"I told him about you. I thought you were one of his disciples and I mentioned seeing you. If I hadn't…you would be safe."

"For now, until he found me, or someone else saw what I could do and told him. You didn't do this to me," Sayah said with passion in her voice. "You can't claim ownership for your father or his decisions, no matter how much you want to."

"There are so many other things I would rather do," Kage said, resting one hand on the brick wall beside her and moving his body a hair closer to hers. He wrapped his other arm around her and gently rubbed her back.

He shouldn't stand so close to me, she thought. *If someone saw us... Hell, what do I care if someone sees us? Nobody notices me anyway. He's so close that I can feel his heart beating like it's inside my chest. Surely that...* All thought fled her mind as the heat of his body drove her to distraction.

"Please," she said, her voice quiet. "Could you please step back a bit? I could use some space." She looked up at him, her lips slightly parted and he sighed, stepping back from her.

His heart skipped a beat as she threw herself forward again, wrapping her arms around him in a tight hug. "But I thought—"

She interrupted him, pressing her lips against his before she could change her mind again. He pulled her closer and deepened the kiss, plundering the sweet softness of her mouth and dancing his tongue along hers. He felt his body react to her and knew she felt the pressure of him too, but he dug his hands into her hair, liberating a few of her pins in his effort to hold her even closer to him.

Sayah reached up, threading her fingers through his hair and running them down the back of his neck and along his shoulders. Kage bit back a moan at the sensation of her hands on his skin and nipped at her lower lip with his teeth, then licked the spot lightly to soothe her. He slid his tongue along hers and she latched on, gently pulling on it. She squirmed against him, her hands running down his back and pulling on his hips.

"Too many layers of clothes. Why does society insist we wear so many layers of clothes?" he muttered to himself as he disentangled their bodies and adjusted his breeches.

Sayah's lips were swollen and ruby red from his kiss, and she was delightfully disheveled where his hands had pulled strands of hair from her pins and grasped the fabric of her dress, wrinkling it and pulling the tucked bodice partially free. Her eyes, vague and unfocused, had darkened to a tumultuous deep blue that reminded him of the seas described in pirates' tales. A soft hum came from her throat as she carefully pushed strands of hair behind her ears and back into the twist of hair, then tucked her bodice back into place.

"Oh? Huh?" she said. "Were you talking to me?"

"A bit distracted, are we, dearie?"

Sayah blushed crimson and looked away. "Of course not," she said. "I just wasn't listening to a word you said."

He slid a finger down the side of her face where it met the delicate curve of her ear, then gently caressed her jaw. "Oh love, don't worry about it. Shall we go back to The Rusty Pig?"

"Yes," she said softly. "I feel like this has been enough craziness for the day." She stood on the tips of her toes and brushed a kiss against his cheek. "Let's go back to the Pig."

CHAPTER SEVENTEEN

"They're staying at The Rusty Pig," Maddox said as he paced the floor in front of Dal'gon's massive carved teak desk in the office he kept off the main hall of the brothel. "I caught a glimpse of them at Madame Archambault's place in the merchant district this afternoon, as well. It appears that Kage has taken a liking to the chit." He glanced at him out of the corner of his eye, waiting for his reaction.

"All the better. It will be an adequate punishment for him when I take her away from him," Dal'gon said, his voice icy cold as he rested his steepled hands on his desk before him. His eyes narrowed, focused on Maddox's face. "Have they been intimate?"

"I can't be sure, but I don't believe so. Her soul still appears pure. Kage shielded her as soon as he sensed me, so I wasn't able to get a good look at her. And when I tested him in the alley after they left the *modiste*, he took lashes from my shadow whip and kept his body curled around hers to protect her." Maddox jumped as a vase crashed into the wall behind him.

"This is an interesting development." Dal'gon's face remained impassive, but the flames behind his irises flared. Danger echoed within his tone. "It will go badly for him if he spoils her."

Gooseflesh rose on Maddox's arms at Dal'gon's tone of voice, and he studied his face carefully to ascertain "Where should we go from here?" He asked quietly, trying to avoid angering his father further. "What's our next move?"

"You are truly useless, aren't you? Leave me be," Dal'gon said. He turned away from Maddox, shadows rippling around him. "Begone."

Maddox nodded, bowing slightly, and exited the chamber to descend the spiral staircase to the family quarters. Dal'gon locked the door and sealed the lock with a knot of shadows, then sat heavily in the armchair near the fire. He crossed his legs, throwing one ankle onto his opposing knee, and stared into the flames, his face contorted with rage. The logs in the fireplace crackled and snapped as he threw the glass of bourbon into the fire. He hissed as smoke billowed into the room.

"The fool," Dal'gon said as he watched the flames burn off the alcohol. "Thinking he can outwit me, taking the girl from under my nose. But how will I respond…" He drummed his fingers against his thigh, losing himself in his thoughts. The crackling flame mesmerized him, allowing him to clear his mind of other distractions.

"I suppose… oh yes, that could work. Especially now that we know where he is hiding."

~

"He's right unhinged," Maddox said to Reisu as they walked through the dimly lit hallway outside his room. He turned to look at her and smirked, leaning casually against the wall. He reached out to grasp a tendril of her hair that had come loose from her chignon, tucking it back behind her ear.

"More so than usual, you mean?" she asked, a faint blush on her cheeks. "He's been downright pleasant to the girls the past few days, which is...out of character." She trailed a finger down his arm, hooking it into the leather bracelet at his wrist. She tugged gently and smiled up at him.

"His obsession with Kage's little tart could be the downfall of us all." He stopped outside the door to his chambers and turned. "Would you care to join me for a nightcap?"

Reisu nodded, following him into the room. The door closed behind them with a quiet click.

CHAPTER EIGHTEEN

B ess gasped as Sayah walked through the kitchen door. "Oh my gods," she said. "Oh my gods." She ran to Sayah, wrapping her in an embrace, then leaned back to admire the delicately woven fabric. "Oh, this fabric is divine. The cotton is so soft that it's almost silken."

"Is that a good thing?" Kage asked.

"Yes," Sayah said, laughing. "It's a very good thing." She spun in a circle for Bess, her skirts swishing around her ankles, then showed off the matching slippers. "Aren't they beautiful?"

"Yes," Bess exclaimed, squealing. "And the hat. The hat! Wow. What's a girl gotta do to get you to buy her pretty things?" she asked Kage.

Kage's jaw dropped and he stared at Bess, mute. He opened and closed his mouth a few times, confusion in his eyes. The girls looked at each other and grinned, bursting into hysterical laughter.

"I'm just joking," Bess said between giggles. "I wasn't implying..." she trailed off as great gales of laughter shook her shoulders.

"Let's just pretend that none of what just happened... happened, shall we?" Kage said, blushing furiously.

Sayah and Bess burst into fits of giggles again at the awkwardness of his statement, holding onto one another and shaking with laughter. Kage shook his head and sat down at the table beside the fire, putting his feet up on the hearth.

"It's fine, I'll wait," he said, inspecting his cuticles and pretending to be unaffected by their hysterics.

Sayah took a deep breath and looked away for a moment, staring into the flames and steadying herself, then joined Kage at the kitchen table. Bess walked to the wide counter where the bread dough was rising and punched it down, forming it into individual loaves and lining them up on trays. She covered each loaf individually, the sackcloth towels holding in warmth, and focused on the automatic motions to settle herself from the giggle fit she and Sayah had shared. When the work was finished, she turned around and smiled at them both.

"Okay, I think I'm calm now," she said, wiping the flour from her hands. "Your dress is beautiful, Sayah."

"Thank you," Sayah replied, smiling. "I'm so happy that Madame Archambault had one made that she could take in for me."

"Madame Archambault?" Bess asked, her eyebrows shooting up toward her hairline. "She's the best modiste in Ship's Haven."

"That's what I had heard," Kage said. "My father's *majordomo* speaks very highly of her skill with a needle and thread."

"His *majordomo*?" Sayah asked.

"Yes. She runs his household, brothel, and manages all of his affairs so that he can remain 'a man of leisure.' Her name is Reisu."

"Reisu," Bess repeated softly. "I knew a Reisu once, years and years ago. She disappeared when we were young girls, maybe six or seven years old."

"It couldn't possibly be the same person; perhaps a distant relative, as it is an uncommon name," Kage said. "Reisu has been with my father for at least two centuries. The disappearance is strange, though."

"Centuries?" Sayah asked.

"Yes. When I found you, you were reading about him in that book at the library. You know that he's been around for almost a millenia; they mention it in that book." Kage shrugged. "I try not to think about it too much. It's a hard concept to wrap your mind around."

"So you're my age, but he's a thousand years old, and she's been with him for centuries, so that would mean his *majordomo* is hundreds of years old, too. She's not..." she trailed off.

"Not human, yes. Reisu is a wraith. She can take corporeal form if she wishes to, but she prefers to appear as wisps of smoke in the shape of a woman."

"Wisps of smoke," Sayah said, turning the thought over in her head. "The first night I saw you, when I followed you —I thought you were talking to yourself in the alley, but there were clouds of smoke around you. You were talking to her."

"Yes," Kage said. "We were discussing how angry my father would be that I was coming home smelling like cheap beer and tavern girls."

Sayah cringed, remembering all the crude things said to the serving girls in the taproom. "Tavern girls? You like to dally with tavern girls?"

"No." Kage laughed. "I would pour beer on myself at whatever place I was hiding out for the night and make myself appear rumpled so that he would believe I had been out wenching."

"If you weren't actually out drinking and carousing, then what were you doing?"

"Reading in the library, visiting students at the Lyceum who study philosophy and ancient religions for debates, walking along the canals that lead down to the dock district... Sometimes I would sit in taverns and listen to old men tell stories of their days in the military and fighting battles on foreign soil." Kage sighed, his eyes appearing distant as he thought back to his nights of quiet rebellion. "Sometimes I would just find a quiet place to sit and watch the waves lap against the shore so that I could find some semblance of peace in the quiet splashing of the water against the sand. Anything, really, because I didn't want to be home, surrounded by the sounds of my father's brothel and the angry voices of my brothers as they argued over which of them is the superior hunter."

Sayah frowned. "But he thought you were out doing gods knew what, any manner of sin, when really you were learning and growing. Making yourself a better person, a better man."

He nodded, a serious look on his face. "I have no desire to fight with my brothers over who is the best errand boy for my father, and I refuse to embrace the demonic part of my soul. So I hid myself as best I could and cultivated the reputation of a ne'er do well womanizer so that they would leave me alone. Until I saw you."

"Me?"

"When I saw you, swirling in the shadows in that alley, I knew I had to report you to him. He has ways of telling when we omit something from our reports, and all of us are required to report back to him whenever we return from the city. To hide something from him...the consequences could be anything, fully dependent on his whims. Any sightings of someone who can use the shadows that way must be reported immediately so that he can have someone, usually Maddox, investigate." He paused. "Please don't be upset with me, but I reported you to him and, when he said he was going to send someone after you, I volunteered. He believed I was finally interested in participating in our endeavors and agreed." He looked at Sayah cautiously.

"I-I won't be upset. But why would you agree to come after me when you know that he will hurt me?"

"Because the alternative was Maddox, and I knew that you would recognize me as the person who saved you. I hoped that would make it easier for me to get to you, and I knew that I could ensure you wouldn't be hurt if I was with you. Whereas with Maddox…I had no guarantees." Kage reached for Sayah's hand and gripped it gently, caressing the back of her hand with his thumb. "I didn't know you then, but I knew that I wasn't going to let you be hurt if you were truly an innocent in all of this."

"You agreed to chase after me to protect me?" Sayah looked incredulous.

"This sounds like a load of horse shit to me," Bess growled, stepping closer to Sayah. "You just admitted that you're the one who turned her in and offered to hunt her, but not for your own glory, you were being noble by hunting her yourself? You expect us to believe that crap?"

"I swear it on my mother's grave. I didn't know you yet, but something about your eyes made me— I don't know. I just knew that I didn't want Maddox to catch you. I wanted you to be safe."

"On your mother's grave? Your mother is dead?" Bess asked, her tone softening slightly though a scowl continued to wrinkle her freckled skin.

"Yes— birthing a hybrid is no easy process, and Father didn't— well, I suppose he didn't care if his breeding stock survived or not, once they fulfilled their purpose. She managed to live for a few weeks, but she was severely depleted after my birth and didn't receive any sort of medical intervention. One afternoon her heart just…stopped." Kage looked away before they could see the tears forming in his eyes. "Reisu found her that way, with me laying in her arms, and made the decision to take care of me after that, though she had no idea what to do with a newborn. When I was older, she told me what happened."

A single tear fell from Sayah's eyes, and she wiped it away impatiently. "Thank you," she said, her voice solemn. "For sharing that part of yourself with us."

"You're welcome," Kage said. He raised her hand and brought it to his lips, gently kissing her knuckles. "I'm sorry that I had to report you, but I can't be sorry that it led me here. To this place, eating fantastic beef pie, with you."

Bess cleared her throat loudly, looking between Kage and Sayah in amusement and frustration. "I hate to interrupt, but," she said, "I need to get prepping for dinner before the taproom fills up with hungry mouths in need of bread and stew."

"And ale," Kage said. "You can't forget the ale."

Sayah rolled her eyes. "Is there anything I can do to help, Bess?"

"Get out of my hair for a bit so that I can cook, then come down later and we'll have a pint and some stewed beef tips." She gestured toward the small staircase that led to the rooms above the tavern. "Now, out with you lot before I lose my mind from your mooning over each other."

CHAPTER NINETEEN

Kage turned the key and opened the door for Sayah, following her into their suite. He could smell her, the scent of honey and lavender with a hint of lemon floating past him as she walked by. She set her hat carefully on the little table beside the settee, arranging the ribbons just so to ensure they wouldn't crease. She kicked off her slippers and sat down on the settee, curling her feet under her and arranging her skirts. Kage slipped off his jacket, throwing it over the back of the chair beside the fire, and loosened his cravat. He sat down opposite Sayah, lounging with one leg thrown over the arm of the wingback chair. She stared at him, her lips slightly parted. He grinned at her.

"What's on your mind?" he asked.

"Your mother," Sayah said quietly, pulling her knees up to her chest and wrapping her arms around them.

"My mother?"

"Yes. You never got to know her…I know what that's like. I have almost no memory of the beforetimes, and the few memories I do have don't tell me much of anything about my mother." Sayah paused, taking a deep breath. "I wish you had the chance to know her. I wish we both had the chance to grow up with our mothers."

"I do too," Kage said. "But the benefit of all this false debauchery is that I've had a great deal of time to think. I've learned that there are some things in my life that I can't control. So I focus on what I can."

"And what is that?" Sayah asked. "Your father believing that you're a leach?"

"My father remaining unaware of my attempts to improve myself so that I can eventually get out from under his thumb forever. That's been all I've wanted for a very long time. And what about you?" Kage asked, studying her face. "What do you want now that you've begun to learn about your abilities?"

She licked her lips, a faint blush forming on her cheeks, and smiled as she watched his pupils dilate. "You," she said.

Kage growled his approval and leapt, jumping across the table and onto the settee. He grabbed her waist and pulled her toward him, sending the small table careening to the side as her skirts swung out. She hoisted them to her knees and pushed the voluminous layers of fabric out of the way so she could straddle him, diving her fingers into his thick hair and weaving them through the silken strands as he lurched up to capture her lips with his. He dug his fingers into her hips, pulling her tightly to him, and moved his hands up her back to the buttons that lined the dress along her spine. Sayah parted her lips and slid her tongue along his lower lip, nipping it with her teeth as he worked to slip each button free from its adjoining loop.

"So many buttons," Kage said, pulling his lips from hers and peering over her shoulder, struggling to free another one from its loop. "Why do dresses have so many damned buttons?" He danced his fingers down her spine as he slid the top of her dress free from her shoulders. He kissed his way down her cheek to her neck, gently running his lips and teeth down the delicate skin behind her ear toward the gentle slope of her shoulder.

"More," she said as he raked his teeth across the sensitive spot of skin just above her collarbone. She tilted her head to the side to give him better access. "Oh gods, yes."

He lifted his mouth from her neck and smiled wolfishly. "You taste like the breeze coming off the ocean on a warm summer night."

She looked at him, starry eyed. "I don't know what to say," she said, her voice heavy with passion.

"You don't have to say anything at all," Kage said. He kissed the tip of her nose, making her giggle. "Sayah."

"Kage," she said, mimicking the serious tone of his voice.

"Do you want to keep going?" he asked. "We can stop if you want to."

She stared at him for a moment, stunned, then reached forward and grabbed his face, pulling his lips to hers for a quick kiss. "I don't ever want to stop kissing you."

Kage grinned at her, reaching up to caress her cheek. She leaned her face against his hand, then turned to kiss his palm, flicking her tongue over it lightly. He moved his hand back into her hair, pulling her face toward his. She sighed into his mouth and he pulled her closer, angling her back onto the settee and sliding her beneath him. His hand slid up her leg to her thigh, unhooking the garter that held up her stocking and sliding the silk down her skin. A shiver ran down her spine at the gentle touch of his hands on her bare skin. He slid her skirts higher, trailing his fingers along the sensitive skin of her inner thighs and up to the waist of her bloomers. She moaned, and he stiffened at the sound. He hooked a finger into the waistband and stopped, pulling his lips from hers.

"Is this okay?" he asked.

"Yes," Sayah said. She grasped his free hand and held it against her heart. "Kage, don't stop."

He groaned, dipping his fingers beneath the waistband and teasing the soft skin of her belly. Her soft sigh reverberated through his body and he stopped, staring at the line of pale skin below the bottom of her corset. He leaned back, pulling her with him, and finished undoing the buttons down the back of her dress, sliding it the rest of the way off of her torso. She stood and he pulled the dress from her hips and undid her petticoats. He held her hand as she stepped free of the pile of clothing, standing before him in her bloomers, shift, and corset. He knelt before her, kissing the delicate skin of her thigh before standing to lead her to his bedroom.

He held her hand as they walked through the door to the bedroom, then swung her up into his arms. She wrapped her arms around his neck and he kissed her as he carried her to the bed. He set her carefully onto the thick mattress, her dark curls tumbling down her bare arms and back, contrasting with her pale skin and the ivory muslin of her corset. Her breasts heaved as she watched him study her, the deep turquoise of her eyes mirroring the emotions he felt.

"Are you cold?" he asked, noticing the gooseflesh on her arms.

"A little," Sayah said, rubbing her hands against her arms.

"I can stoke the fire," he said, gesturing to the small fireplace in the corner of the room. "Or I can get into the bed with you."

She crooked a finger at him and he pounced, pulling his cravat free. She unbuttoned his shirt and nipped the skin just below his collarbone, licking the spot and tasting his skin. She pushed him down onto the mattress, swinging a leg over him and straddling his hips. Her breasts spilled over the top of the corset, affording him a teasing glimpse of rosy nipples against her porcelain skin. He reached a hand up to touch her, but she grabbed his wrist and pinned it to the bed. Kissing him deeply, she moved against him, reveling in the feel of his hard body beneath hers.

"The way you feel," she said between kisses, "is unlike anything I've ever felt before."

Kage looked up into her eyes, feeling his heartbeat race in time with hers. "Tell me what you feel."

"I feel power. Strength. The lines of your muscles belie your scholarly endeavors; I can tell that you spend time in the boxing ring. You have the scars to prove it, and your nose is a little crooked." She kissed its tip and smiled. "I feel your length pressed against me, hard and thick. I feel the calluses of your hands scraping against my skin when you stroke your hands over me. I feel everything."

"Everything?"

"I feel like I truly belong for the first time in—" Sayah cut off as a shadow twitched in the corner of the room, shifting. "What was—"

"Bravo, little brother," a voice said from the shadows. "You've got her right where Father wants her. In bed." Maddox stepped fully into the room, the glow of the fire casting dancing shadows across his skin.

"Maddox?" Kage's voice was hostile, and he grasped Sayah's hand tightly as he sat up in the bed. "What the hell are you doing here?"

"Come now, little brother, you really ought to check your wards before you get…distracted. Don't play coy. You know why I'm here." He smirked, twisting a whip of shadow and flame around his hand. "Give me the girl."

"I can't do that," Kage said. "She's not mine to give."

The whip cracked into the ceiling, dropping a fine dust of

plaster from the ceiling like rain. "Don't be an idiot. You know that Father won't stop until he has her under his control. Give her to me so that we can stop this ridiculous farce of a rebellion against him." Maddox took a menacing step forward, readying the whip for another strike.

"No," Sayah said firmly. "Kage is right. It's not his decision to give me over to you. It's mine, and I will not go."

"Pathetic little girl, trying to be brave. You smell just like your mother—like ocean breezes and sunshine. She was delicious," Maddox said. "Well, if you're sure…So be it." He flicked his wrist and bands of shadow grabbed her ankles, binding her. He pulled her from the bed in one swift tug, spilling her to the floor.

Kage growled low in his throat and leapt from the bed, but Maddox was ready for the attack. A spear of shadow appeared in his hand and pierced Kage's shoulder, wringing a pained scream from him. He fell to the ground, blood flowing freely from the wound as Maddox bound Sayah's wrists behind her back and threw her over his shoulder.

"Father says to ensure that you are home within the hour," Maddox said as he turned his back on Kage. "He wants you there when he enjoys the spoils of your little rebellion. Failure to return will result in consequences."

"What else could he possibly do to me?" Kage asked.

"Not to you," Maddox said, malice in his voice. "That would be rather anticlimactic after this, no? It's what he will do to the girl that will be your punishment." With that, he twisted the shadows and stepped into the shadow realm with Sayah over his shoulder.

Kage leaned against the wall and stared at the corner where they had disappeared for what felt like hours, pressing the remnant of his shirt to his shoulder tightly to staunch the bleeding. As the blood flow slowed and his dizziness subsided, he took a deep breath and sat up fully.

"Okay," he said to himself as he braced himself against the wall and struggled to his feet. "It's time to come up with a plan."

CHAPTER TWENTY

K age ran down the stairs, his bloody, tattered shirt around his shoulders. He burst into the kitchen.

Bess turned to scold him, then saw his face. "What? What's happened? Where is Sayah?"

"Maddox," Kage said, anger and fear filling his voice. His hands shook. "Maddox took her from me." He stumbled to the chair by the fire and collapsed into it, his shirt falling open to reveal the wound.

"She…wait. Your brother took her. From here. From your rooms?" Bess paced around the kitchen, wringing her hands.

"Plucked her out of my arms as we were… well, that doesn't matter overmuch. He took her from me, and my father demands that I arrive home within the hour."

"When? How long ago?"

"I'm not sure," Kage said. "He stabbed me with a spear of shadow, and I lost some time while I tried to staunch the bleeding."

Bess looked at him, as though seeing the bloody, tattered shirt for the first time. "Ok, you went upstairs about 45 minutes ago, so…"

"I should go. I have to go right away. He said…Bess, they will hurt her to punish me if I don't get there on time."

"Go," Bess said, pushing him out the kitchen door and into the alley. "Bring her home."

Sayah stared out the window that overlooked the harbor, high enough above the dock district that she could almost imagine she was somewhere else. Maddox had placed her in a different chamber this time, rather than Kage's old room, and she felt disoriented by the dramatic difference in the decor. Where Kage's former bedroom had held a sense of old world charm and well-loved coziness, this room possessed an entirely different feel. Filled with gilt mirrors and a gleaming metal four poster bed, the decor was gaudy and uncomfortable, more suitable for a drama being performed at the theater than a bedroom. The walls were papered with crimson silk with a floral motif, the delicate fabric tinting the light in the room red. She shivered slightly at the draft coming in through the gaps around the window frame and turned, searching for the dressing gown she had noticed on the back of a nearby chair.

"Feathers," she mumbled as she pulled the garment around her shoulders. "It's trimmed in feathers." She shook her head, torn between disgust and amusement at the gaudy trim. She wrapped the satin robe tighter around her body, desperate for warmth and trying to ignore the tickle of the feathers against her face and neck. She glanced at the clock on the mantle. "How has it only been five minutes?"

She turned back to the window and watched the water in the distance. The sunlight rippled across the surface of the waves, painting them with dappled light as they ebbed and flowed. She breathed in time with the gently rushing of the waves, willing herself into a trance-like state.

A small crackling noise from the far corner of the room broke her focus, drawing her attention. She whipped her head around, startled, as Dal'gon entered the room, emerging from the depths of the shadows cast by the late afternoon sun, followed closely by Maddox and Reisu.

"Sayah. Say-yuh," Dal'gon said slowly, as though savoring the taste of her name on his tongue. He strode across the room and grabbed her arm, pulling her away from the window. He grasped a handful of her hair, forcing her head back to stare into her eyes for a moment. The flames crackled and popped in the fireplace as he pushed her into a chair beside it. Bands of shadow snapped from him, securing her ankles and waist to the chair. "Yes, that will do," he said smugly, ravishing her with his eyes.

Sayah squirmed, testing the strength of the bindings, but refused to look him in the eye again. He grasped her chin tightly and lifted her face so that she was unable to look at anything but him. Color rose in her cheeks and her eyes flashed with temper as he held her there, refusing to allow her to look away. She narrowed her eyes and spat at him. He released her chin and wiped the glob of saliva from his face.

"That was a mistake, little girl," Maddox said.

Dal'gon's hand whipped out, striking her across the face. Her head snapped back from the impact and her vision blurred. The chair tipped backward, toppling her to the side. She lay there, stunned.

"Do you see what you've made me do, insolent child? You're bleeding all over my Aubusson rug." Dal'gon flexed his fingers as he glared at her.

Sayah sat up in silence. A trickle of blood dribbled from her nose from the slap, but she ignored it. As her vision returned to normal, she maintained eye contact with Dal'gon and kept her face clear of any emotion.

Maddox walked over to Dal'gon and leaned close to him. "Perhaps you shouldn't strike her, Father. When Kage gets here…"

Dal'gon cut him off. "When Kage gets here," he said, "he will do as he's told for once. Regardless of what he thinks he deserves to do. I owe him nothing."

"Of course, Father, I apologize for suggesting that—"

"Cease your endless noise, Maddox. Your voice grates on my ears." Dal'gon flexed his hands, tightening the bands around Sayah's ankles and waist. "Now, Sayah, I very much wish to hear from you—what were you and my son doing?"

"I'm afraid I don't know what you mean," Sayah said. "What were we doing when Maddox kidnapped me? Or what were we doing together at The Rusty Pig?" She shrugged, full of disdain. "You're being needlessly vague, and it's a waste of my time."

"You're an insolent little idiot, aren't you? Your time means nothing. Just a silly little mortal who will never amount to anything." Dal'gon watched her face as he spoke, waiting for any sign of weakness to appear. "Don't trifle with me, girl. What were you and my son doing?"

"Well, I should think my attire when Maddox brought me here would be a rather significant clue. We had just gone into Kage's bedroom and he had thrown me onto the—"

"Enough." Dal'gon's voice was hard.

"Oh no, Dal'gon, it wasn't nearly enough. We had only just begun. I don't think I could ever get my fill of him." Sayah smirked at him, taking immense pleasure in the anger flashing in his eyes. "Oh, is that not what you meant? Forgive me."

"You have to have been plotting something. There is no

other reason for him to steal you from me," Dal'gon said. "What were you planning?"

"Truthfully? He couldn't steal me because I was never yours to begin with. Regardless, our only plan was to learn where my powers came from," she said truthfully. "Anything else that came from that would have been inconsequential."

"Your powers," Dal'gon said, turning the idea over in his mind. "My son agreed to help you discover the origin of your ability to manipulate shadows?"

"Yes," Sayah said. "He volunteered, actually. Something you said to him when he brought me here caught his interest and he wanted to explore it."

"Something about your lineage, I assume," Dal'gon said, sitting down in the chair opposite her. He gestured to Reisu and Maddox, beckoning them to come and join them. "Reisu, what was it that you said about Sayah's lineage when you saw her the first time?"

"She has been angel-kissed," Reisu replied. "Either her mother or father was part angel. Well, that would be my guess, at least."

"So," Dal'gon said to Sayah, "which was it? Your mother or your father?"

"I'm afraid I don't understand what you mean," Sayah said, trying to feign ignorance.

"Which of your parents was it, Sayah? Which one was able to do extraordinary things?" Reisu asked, leaning forward from where she sat.

"My mother," she said, "though I didn't know it until recently. My memories of the beforetimes are hazy, at best. I only recently began to regain some of them."

Dal'gon tapped the tips of his fingers against his thigh, staring at Sayah. The intensity of his gaze sent a chill down her spine, but she carefully controlled her features to appear unaffected.

"The beforetimes. What a quaint way to refer to your childhood," Reisu said. "Before what?"

"Before your boss ordered my parents killed," Sayah said, turning her glare to Reisu. "Before Maddox held my mother by the throat and drained the blood from her over my father's corpse while I hid from him and his lackeys."

Reisu looked between Maddox and Dal'gon. Her face betrayed no emotion, but the focused look she gave them seemed to speak volumes. Maddox shrugged slightly, though he wilted under her gaze.

Maybe, Sayah thought, *she didn't know what she has aligned herself with.*

Dal'gon winked at Reisu and reached out, tickling the wisps of smoke that made up her hands.

"Yes, I thought you smelled familiar," Maddox said. "Your mother...her spirit was delicious. Like honey drizzled on a warm scone."

Pain filled Sayah's eyes as the memory of her mother's death floated to the forefront of her mind again.

Reisu watched her, curious about the myriad of emotions that crossed her face. "This is still a fresh wound for you," Reisu said. "Interesting."

"Interesting?" Sayah repeated. "You think the murder of my parents for gods know what reason is interesting?" She flexed her ankles, trying to loosen the bonds of shadow that held her, but they wouldn't give way.

Dal'gon chuckled quietly. He stood and walked to her, kneeling before her and parting her robe to gaze upon her breasts, thrust high above her corset. "Would you like to know why your parents were killed, Sayah?" he asked as he stroked a hand down her arm. "Would you like to know why my men stopped hunting you after they were eliminated?"

Sayah glared at him in response.

"For you, little fool. They were killed to get to you. They stopped hunting because you disappeared and they couldn't trace you. Now, of course, we know why—that you have abilities with shadow that are completely untraceable—but we didn't know that at the time."

"No," she said. "No. That can't be true." Her body shook as waves of grief and rage crashed over her. "Why would you kill them to get to me? I was just a little girl." She looked away, tears threatening to overwhelm her from the grief of the new wounds Dal'gon ripped into her psyche.

"Your mother's purity and strength of spirit, your father's intelligence and cunning, combined in you. The angel blood you inherited from your mother made you unique, but your aptitude for shadow manipulation, despite your lack of demon blood...that truly separated you from the other angelic brethren in Ship's Haven." He grasped her chin hard, forcing her to look at him again. "These abilities have never been seen in someone without demon blood. Someone without my blood. Yet you possessed them, even then," he stressed.

"How did you—" Sayah's voice cracked and she stopped before finishing her thought.

"The shadows answer to me. They whispered to me of a girl with immense power who could wield both the darkness and the light." Dal'gon watched her closely, gauging her reaction.

"You have no right to be able to control the shadows the way you do," Maddox said, cutting into the conversation. "None. You are not part of the family."

"Maddox, stop," Reisu said. "Let your father educate the chit."

Dal'gon loosened his grip on her chin slightly, staring at her lips before continuing. "With your strength and angelic blood, I can sire a child unlike any other. The combination of angelic and demonic blood will create a hybrid human that will be capable of overthrowing any government, assassinating any leader, dominating any culture."

"No." Sayah shook her head. "I won't. Not interested."

"You will. And you will like it, or I will force you to like it." Dal'gon stood, releasing the bands of shadow that bound her.

Sayah fell to the floor, her legs giving way beneath her as she panicked. "No. No…Please. Gods no, I can't." Dark laughter filled her ears.

"Pick a god and pray to it, if that will make you feel better. It's not going to change anything. The gods can't help you now." Maddox smirked. "Father will have you. One way or another."

CHAPTER TWENTY-ONE

D arkness lingered in every corner of the room, but the shadows no longer offered comfort. Sayah lay on the bed, curled beneath the opulent satin bedspread with her head pillowed on her arms. Sobs shook her shoulders as Dal'gon's threats weighed on her mind. A soft noise drew her attention and she raised her head.

"Shush," Kage said quietly as he sat on the bed beside her. He pulled her into his arms and wiped the tears from her eyes. "Don't cry, love."

Sayah rested her cheek against his chest, wrapping her arms around his back. "Did you know?" she asked.

"Know what?"

"That your father killed my parents because he wanted me." She tilted her head back to look at him. "Did you know?"

"No. He never said…he just planted the seed about angelic blood being an explanation for your abilities and left it there."

"He wants me to…to…" She stopped, unable to finish her sentence.

"To what?"

"He wants me to breed him another heir. A child who would be capable of toppling dynasties and creating mayhem."

Kage's eyes flashed. "He wants you to bear him a child," he said, anger simmering in his words. "He wants to use you—"

"Maddox killed my parents so that I wouldn't be protected. So that I would be alone," she said, ending on a sob. "Don't you see what that means?"

"Tell me." Kage stroked his hand up and down her arm as he held her.

"He always knew I was out there. When you came to him, he knew exactly who I was. And he wanted you to find me. He wanted you to bring me here to him so that he could finally get what he wants most of all." She slumped back into the bed, her shoulders shaking from her desperate effort to hold back her tears. "Me."

Kage curled up behind her, wrapping his arms around her. "I had no idea. I'm so sorry, Sayah. I led him to you." His face fell and he buried it in her shoulder, inhaling the soft scent that clung to her skin. "I have to go," he said. "I snuck up here after I saw Father, but I'm expected to be seated at dinner when he brings you down. My punishment for disobeying him is to be forced to watch you with him."

"Please," Sayah begged. "Please don't let him touch me."

"If I can find a way to get us out of here, I will," Kage said. "But he barricaded the door we snuck out of last time, and he took my ability to walk in the shadow realm, so we can't escape that way."

"Kage, I—" She rolled over, facing him.

"Don't," he said, gently pressing his lips to her cheek. "You don't need to say anything. I know."

"I need to say it," Sayah said. "I need to tell you. I…I love you, Kage."

A smile teased up the corners of his lips, and he cupped her chin gently, tilting her head back to kiss her softly on the lips. "I know," he said. "I love you, too. I will find a way to get us out of here. I won't let him touch you."

"Promise?"

"I promise," he said solemnly.

The hinges creaked as the dining room door swung open. Kage looked up from his spot at the far end of the table, distant candlelight dancing across the planes of his face. As Reisu swept through the door in her corporeal form, she smirked at him.

"Kage, you've returned to the fold," she said as settled into the chair he pulled out for her. "Still wenching and drinking cheap ale, or has the chit upstairs changed you?"

"No woman could change me," Kage said, his voice filled with false bravado. "I am who I have always been. Cheap ale, tavern wenches, and all."

"Then let me pour you a glass of your father's excellent wine while we wait for the rest of the dinner guests to arrive. I know it's not the same quality of beverage you're used to, but I'm sure it will suffice." She floated over to the sideboard and poured two glasses of deep burgundy wine and carried one to him. "So tell me, what was it like?"

"What was what like?" he asked.

"What was it like to be out from under your father's thumb for the first time?"

"I wasn't aware that I was out from under his thumb at all. It seems as though all of this was meticulously planned."

Bitterness seeped into Kage's voice, despite his best efforts to keep a flippant tone.

"Oh no," Reisu said. "This has not gone according to plan at all. Dal'gon never intended for you to fall in love with the girl."

"That makes two of us, then." He took a long gulp of the wine, wincing slightly at the burn in the back of his throat.

"The things I could tell you…" She trailed off, staring at the flickering candles.

"I'm sure you have plenty of stories about him that I don't want to hear," Kage said. "But isn't all of that beside the point? I'm sure Father and Maddox will be escorting our guest down shortly."

"It's true, then," Reisu said as she watched the myriad emotions flickering across his face. "You really do love her."

"Of course I love her," Kage replied. "Why else would I have put myself between her and Maddox when he came at us in the alley?"

"I had wondered. But then he managed to take her from you."

"If he hadn't come after her while we were becoming… better acquainted, he wouldn't have gotten the jump on me. As soon as her lips were on mine, I stopped being able to focus on the shadows in the room. Wait," he said suddenly. "Why am I even telling you this? It's not like you care."

"Because you need someone to help you, and I've always been the one to get you out of scrapes in the past." Reisu took a deep breath, steadying herself. "I don't think I can get you out of this one, Kage, even if I wanted to. He wants your blood, but he wants to torture you first."

"I don't care. She was worth it," he said. "She is worth it."

Footsteps sounded on the polished hardwood floors of the

hallway, announcing Maddox's arrival. He carried Sayah's unconscious form in his arms, her head lolling back. He set her in a chair, folding her forward so that her head rested against the table in front of her, her loose curls spilling down into her lap.

"What the hell did you do to her?" Kage shouted, rage filling him. He stood and lunged for his brother, but Reisu grabbed his arm.

"Me? Nothing," Maddox said. "Father sedated her so that we would have less of a fight bringing her down to dinner. She was spitting like a hellcat when he went to her room to fetch her. She'll wake soon."

"Kage," Reisu said. "Sit down. Dal'gon is coming."

Kage sat down again, raking a hand through his hair as he glared at Maddox. Sayah mumbled something incoherently, moving her head to the other side and coughing.. She started to sit up, but fell forward again.

"Mmmph," she said. "Mmmso dizzy."

"You're not making much sense, but I suppose that's the sedative wearing off," Maddox said sardonically. "I can't imagine my brother would have been able to tolerate being around you if you were an absolute dingbat, and you certainly managed to hold your own with Father earlier."

"Ugh," Sayah growned. "My head feels like it's stuffed with lambswool."

"Have a sip of this, it'll help," Reisu said, handing her a glass of cold water. Condensation dripped from the glass, droplets of water staining the fabric of the tablecloth.

Sayah took a sip of the water, letting the cold liquid run down her throat to ease the ache that remained from the sedative, and laid her head back down on the table. Dal'gon strode into the room a moment later and Reisu and Maddox sprang to their feet, bowing slightly at their waists as he approached the table. Kage remained seated, glaring at Dal'gon. His rage shimmered in the darkness of his eyes.

"What is wrong with my prize?" Dal'gon asked, looking at Sayah with curiosity.

"You sedated her and she's having trouble functioning," Kage said with disdain. "You drugged her, Father. What did you expect?"

"Interesting. I haven't seen this type of effect before." Dal'gon studied Sayah's blank expression and groggy eyes with curiosity.

"Congratulations, now you have. She's very clearly still under the influence of whatever you gave her. Can we get this farce over with so that I can go back to my chambers?" Kage drummed his fingers against the tabletop, his irritation bubbling dangerously below the surface.

"Stop," Sayah snapped, her head still flat against the table. "That noise is killing my head. Just be quiet."

Dal'gon pulled out his chair and sat at the head of the table, grabbing the glass of wine that sat beside him. He swished it around the glass, then inhaled deeply, studying the bouquet of the wine. He took a sip and smiled slightly. "Such a nice burgundy," he said conversationally. "You can really taste the chocolate and blackberries. I believe this one is from my own vineyard, is it not, Reisu?"

"Yes, sir. The one on the southern tip of the continent," she replied. "It's a particular favorite of mine. You know how I enjoy blackberries."

"Yes, I recall. And you know how I enjoy sharing my magnificent treasures with guests. Your memory and attention to detail please me," Dal'gon replied. "Tell me, Sayah, do you enjoy wine?"

Sayah groaned in response, her head pillowed on her arms upon the table. A cruel smile twisted Dal'gon's features as he watched her struggle to escape the cocoon the sedatives wrapped her in.

"Maddox, please assist our guest in sitting up so that she can enjoy our hospitality."

Maddox used tendrils of shadow to grab Sayah and secure her in a sitting position. Her head lolled forward when he released it, the sedative's effects lingering far longer than intended. Dal'gon reached for her and took her hand, raising it to his lips. Kage grimaced at the sight, but Reisu put a hand on his arm, stopping him from saying something.

"Shall we eat?" Dal'gon asked, gesturing to the servants alongside the buffet.

CHAPTER TWENTY-TWO

K age picked at the roasted beef and root vegetables, cutting them into smaller pieces and pushing them around the plate to give the appearance that he was eating. Sayah watched him from her seat beside Dal'gon, the bindings around her waist and below her armpits holding her in place and keeping her upright. Her mind still felt fuzzy, despite the food and water they had foisted on her. Her arms hung limply at her sides, too weak to continue lifting the fork to her mouth.

"Tell me, darling, how do you like the roast?" Dal'gon asked.

Kage gripped his fork tightly in his hand, hostility plain on his face.

"It's fine," Sayah said. Her skin crawled at the tone of Dal'gon's voice and the familiarity it implied.

"You haven't eaten in some time. Are you sure it's to your liking?"

"Yes, it's fine. I'm very tired," Sayah said. "My arms feel too heavy to continue eating."

"Allow me to feed you, my dear." Dal'gon lifted a bite of

the roast with a delicate tendril of shadow, pushing it toward her mouth.

Kage gagged at the sight of the meat being forced between Sayah's lips, the tendril of shadow sliding down her chin after depositing the food into her mouth.

"What's the matter, Kage? Is the food not to your liking?" Maddox asked, a sardonic smile on his face.

"It's all a little overdone, don't you think?" Kage said. "I've never been a fan of limp vegetables and dry, stringy roast."

"Come now, that's not very kind of you," Maddox said, looking down to hide the grin on his face. "The cook likely spent hours preparing this feast for us."

"Kindness isn't what we're known for, is it? I know you definitely aren't. And this 'feast' tastes like it was forgotten about in the oven for hours."

"Children," Dal'gon said, his voice commanding. "Cease the arguing this instant. You're ruining the atmosphere."

Kage set his fork down and pushed his chair back from the table, standing. "Good night, Father." He turned on his heel and stormed out of the room, the door slamming in his wake.

Maddox cackled in glee and picked up his wine glass for a toast.

"To my foolish brother and his unceasingly entertaining dramatic exits," he intoned between laughs. "May he—"

"Stop." Dal'gon's voice was stern, leaving no room for argument. A hush fell over the room. "You will stop baiting your brother over his idiocy."

Sayah snapped, her strength returning. She whipped a delicate strand of shadow at Dal'gon, snapping him across the face and leaving a raised welt on his skin. "His what? His idiocy?" she asked, ice in her voice. "Idiocy?" Her voice ended on a preternatural shriek.

Maddox's jaw dropped, and Reisu stood, quickly placing her hand on Dal'gon's arm to restrain him. He threw her hand off of him and breathed deeply, malice flashing in his eyes.

"Are you saying," Sayah asked, "that because Kage has dared to develop feelings for me, he's an idiot? Are you saying that—"

Dal'gon shook his head. "Not at all. I'm saying that he's an idiot for betraying me by stealing you away and failing to hide you both successfully. Because now he will suffer for taking something that belongs to me."

"From you?" Rage painted Sayah's cheeks crimson. She flexed her hands into fists and stretched her mind, popping free of the shadow bindings around her torso. "He stole me from you? You do not own me, Demon. Not you or anyone else. Not Kage. I never belonged to you. I belong only to myself," she spat.

"You possess a piece of my power," Dal'gon said. "Whether you want it or not, you are mine."

"I possess my own power, old man. Or have you truly never considered that shadows do not exist without the light. My power is not the same as yours." She flipped another tendril of shadow at him, but Maddox intercepted it with a shadow of his own. Her shadow rebounded, slapping into her and fastening around her wrist. Another tendril snapped against a pressure point in her neck, dropping her sharply into unconsciousness.

"Keep dreaming," Maddox said snidely.

～

"She's feisty," Reisu whispered to Maddox as they walked from the dining room.

"I can see the appeal." Maddox looked at Sayah appraisingly as Dal'gon carried her unconscious form through the hall. The long ringlets dangled over his father's arm, nearly grazing the floor. "She's not what I expected."

"I agree." Reisu touched Maddox's arm, and he turned to look at her. She traced a line down his arm to his hand and looked up at him from behind her lashes. "Would you care to hunt tonight?" she asked. "It has been some time since you joined me."

"That has great potential, but I may be needed here. Father thinks Kage has some sort of idiocy planned," Maddox said. He placed his hand on her waist and pulled her closer. "It has been entirely too long, though. I will try to escape."

Reisu nipped his ear with her teeth, eliciting a low groan from his throat. "Don't try, just come find me. I'll be waiting."

Sayah snapped back to consciousness as Dal'gon threw her onto the bed in her room.

"Fool," he said, the anger on his face providing a menacing counterpoint to the calmness of his voice. "How dare you defy me before my disciples."

"They aren't disciples, you raging dickweed. They're your children and your major...whatever she is. Your housekeeper."

The back of his hand slammed into her cheek, making her see stars. The skin along her jaw ached, and she could feel a trickle of blood slipping down her face before dripping onto her shoulder. She smiled at him, a devilish light in her eyes.

"Is that all you've got?" she asked, taunting him despite the blood in her mouth. His massive fist hit her square on the nose in answer, knocking her head back. Blood ran freely down her face, but she still smiled.

"Enough." Kage's voice came from the shadows beside the curtained windows. "You will not lay a finger on her again."

"Kage, don't," Sayah pleaded. "I can take it."

"Listen to the girl, Kage."

"You will not touch her again," Kage said.

"So you said, but I can't think of anything you could do to stop me." Dal'gon raised his hand again, stroking it down Sayah's bloody cheek.

Removing a handkerchief from his waistcoat pocket, he dabbed away the blood from her face. His gentleness made Sayah uncomfortable, reminding her too much of the care the butcher gives to a lamb before it is led to slaughter. She shrank back from his ministrations and he grabbed her face, squeezing until he immobilized her. His fingers pinched into her skin, his fingernails carving half moons into her cheeks as he wiped the remaining blood from her face. Seeing Dal'-gon's focus on Sayah, Kage sensed his opening and lunged, throwing bands of shadow at his father. He wrapped the bands around Dal'gon's wrists and ankles, pulling tight and ripping them backwards.

Dal'gon flew back and Kage bound his hands and feet behind his back, hog-tying him.

"Well, Father," he said, "it seems there was something I could do after all." He released Sayah from her bindings and helped her to her feet, then pulled her close to him. He kissed her forehead gently.

She grimaced as she rubbed her wrists, glaring at Dal'gon over Kage's shoulder. She struck him in the face, snapping his head back and dropping him to the floor. "Let's get out of here," she said. "I never want to come here again."

Reisu reformed from the pale wisps of smoke lingering beside the fireplace and stared down at Dal'gon's prone, unconscious body.

"Stupid man," she said. "This is what hubris brings you. Toppled by your son and a girl with angelic blood in her veins." She stepped over him and walked out the door without a backward glance.

She entered her corporeal form and strode through the halls to knock on Maddox's door.

"Enter," he said.

Reisu walked into the room, gray wisps woven around her like swirls of fabric along her skin. "Maddox," she said, her husky voice quiet. "I have news."

"News? We haven't even left the house yet."

"Oh yes," she said. "Big news. Kage has taken the girl. Again."

"What? How?" Maddox raked his fingers through his hair. "There's no way. Father was with her."

"Dal'gon is bound in shadows on the floor of her room," Reisu said. "I watched it all happen in wisp form."

"Well hell," Maddox said. "What were you doing there anyway?"

"He asked me to be in the room, likely to prevent what ended up happening. But she talked back to him, and then he hit her and–" Reisu shrugged. "I decided not to intervene. I suppose that means we have two options," she said. "We can either go release your father and go after Kage now, or we can go hunting as planned and deal with this mess later."

Maddox sighed and stood from his chair. "I guess now is when you tell me that the right thing to do is to go up there and release him? But I think you're forgetting a very viable third option- we use this newfound weakness regarding Sayah to align ourselves against Father and take him out of the equation completely."

"Okay," Reisu said, turning to leave. "So...are we hunting in the dock district, or would you prefer to head up toward the Lyceum and the merchant district?"

"The Lyceum, I think. There are some excellent taverns in that area. We should be able to find something suitable."

CHAPTER TWENTY-THREE

S ayah sat on the edge of Bess' bed, letting her clean the cuts and bruises that decorated her face. Her swollen jaw and nose ached, regardless of the tenderness in Bess' ministrations. Kage paced the floor by the door, cringing at every moan and anguished sound that left Sayah's throat.

"Nearly done," Bess said. She stood and grabbed a small sewing kit from the bedside table and held the needle over the candle flame, sterilizing it. She stitched the deep gash along Sayah's cheekbone, then dabbed it with ointment. "Okay, I think that's it."

"You'll have a scar," Kage said. He cupped her cheek in his hand as he looked down at her.

"Scars aren't a bad thing. I've never understood why women are so desperate to avoid them. They give you character," Sayah said. She tried to smile, but the swelling in her jaw made it difficult to move her lips. One of her eyes was nearly shut, a purple bruise ringing it, and her nose was slightly crooked after the impact.

"You're still beautiful," Kage said. "You will always be

beautiful to me. No matter what my father did." He walked over to the bed and knelt in front of her. Grabbing her hand, he raised her knuckles to his lips. "He won't ruin this for us."

Bess sat down in the chair beside the bed and put her feet up on the feather mattress. "You wouldn't make it as a poet, Kage," she said. "Not even a little bit unique."

Sayah giggled, then winced. "Ugh, everything hurts."

Kage leaned forward and kissed her gently, careful not to put too much pressure on her lips. "I wish I could take your pain away."

"Me too," she said.

"I should go. Father will have people looking for us together. If we split up, it'll be harder for them to find us. We'll both be safer if we're apart for now."

"No, we aren't. We're safer together." Sayah grabbed his hand and held tightly. "Please, Kage. Don't leave."

Kage stared at her. "Okay, but we have to find somewhere else to hide out, and we have to be careful. We can't use the shadows; Father has a way to track us through them."

"Where else could we go?" Sayah asked.

"I have an idea," Bess said. "But you may not like it."

"She was right," Kage said. "I don't like this."

"It really is a good idea," Sayah said. "It's not comfortable, but—"

"I know, I know. I get it." Kage looked around the damp belly of the ship, wrinkling his nose at the scent of mildew and rotting fish that permeated the stale air. "I just wish it didn't smell so bad."

"Three nights here and you're still complaining about the smell. You wouldn't have survived on the streets," Sayah said as she shifted a few barrels around to make a suitable hiding place for their supplies. "The crates and barrels of refuse in the alleys are much worse than this, and there were nights that was the only warmth I could find."

"I… yeah, I'm sure." Kage shuddered. "I probably can't dig my way out of this one, huh?"

"Not if you keep talking, no," Sayah said, laughing. She turned around and grabbed the thin mattress, folding it and placing it on the pile of bedding they kept hidden behind the barrels stored in the ship. "I slept here once, you know, before Bess let me stay with her and you found me at the Lyceum."

"You did?"

"Yes, the night we met," she said. "I had planned to sleep in the captain's quarters, but I ended up in the crew's bunks instead. Running from the men who were after me took a lot more time"

"Then why are we down here?" Kage was taken aback. "You slept in the captain's quarters before, but we're down here in steerage. Below steerage."

"Oh hush."

Kage stretched and walked over to Sayah, gently cupping her cheek. He looked at the stitches and the fading bruises on her face, tracing his fingers carefully over the scar. "I think we can take the stitches out now," he said. "It looks like you're finally healing up."

"Oh good. We'll have to leave a note for Bess so that she can meet us."

"No need," Kage said. He grabbed a small knife from his pocket. "Do you trust me?"

Sayah's eyes widened. "Should I?" she asked, but she sat on a small barrel and looked up at him. "Okay, do it."

Kage carefully slipped the knife beneath each stitch, removing them to reveal the faint discoloration below.

"Barely a scar at all," he said, gently touching the wound. He traced his lips across her cheek, down her jaw, to the sensitive spot on her neck just behind her ear.

A soft moan fluttered from her lips. The silence of the dry docked boat surrounded them; the only sounds they could hear were their quickening breath and pounding hearts. Kage lifted her into his arms and threw her over his shoulder, carrying her up the narrow stairs to the captain's quarters. Her giggle awakened a joy deep within him, and he smiled as he deposited her onto the narrow bed.

"Sayah," he said, savoring the taste of her name on his lips. He leaned forward and captured her mouth with his own, nipping her full lower lip before delving into the sweetness of her mouth with his tongue.

Sayah shivered at the gentle stroke of his tongue against hers, pushing herself closer to him and pulling his shirt free of his breeches. She ran her hands down the taut muscles of his abdomen, a rush of pleasure pulsing through her veins as she felt his muscles flex in response to her touch. "Kage," she whispered between passionate kisses.

He smiled as he lowered his lips to hers again and worked the straps of her thin chemise off of her shoulders. He kissed her shoulder and she shivered, moving her body tight against his. He turned her around, pressing his body against her back as he moved his hands over the bodice of her chemise and the corset below her bust. She pressed herself back against him, his burgeoning hardness twitching against her buttocks as she rubbed against him. He untied the top of the chemise and freed her breasts, filling his hands with them as he made love to her neck with his lips and tongue.

"More," she panted, grasping his hands and holding them tighter to her breasts.

He obliged, drawing lazy circles around her nipples with

his fingertips before gently pinching one, then the other. She moaned low in her throat, and the sound rocked his system, pushing him close to the breaking point. She spun in his arms, wrapping hers around his shoulders and hopping up to wrap her legs around his waist. He put his fingers to work unlacing the corset and freeing her from its confines.

"Sayah," he said, pulling his mouth from hers as his mind cleared. His arms wrapped around her, one hand supporting her bottom. "We should stop. I don't want our first time together to be in this boat, surrounded by moldy fish and gods know what else."

She silenced him with a kiss, pressing her body even closer to his. "I'm sure that I want you," she said. "It doesn't matter where, or when, or how. I want you. Take me to bed, Kage."

"With pleasure," he said as he set her down. He tore the mattress and bedding from where they were stacked behind the barrels and hastily made the bed.

She watched him with amusement in her eyes. At the sound of her chuckle, he turned, and she kept her eyes on his as she slid her chemise off her body. The simple, lace trimmed ivory muslin fell to the floor and pooled at her feet, revealing her curves to his eyes. Her alabaster skin shone in the faint daylight peeking through the porthole on the port side wall.

He strode over to her, stroking his hands over the alabaster skin of her belly. "So soft. So beautiful."

She purred deep in her throat, a satisfied female sound, and reached for the ties that held his breeches. She trailed her fingertips along the soft line of hair that disappeared beneath the waistband, giggling as the flames behind his irises ignited. "More?" she asked innocently.

He grabbed her, pulling her bodily against him, and

lowered her to the bed. Hurriedly divesting himself of his remaining clothes, he moved onto the mattress atop her, finding her mouth with his as his fingers danced over the most sensitive part of her body. Her moan became his music, and he tickled and teased her until she writhed beneath him, arching her hips into his hand, silently begging for more.

Sayah reached for him, grasping his thick manhood and stroking her palm lightly over it. "It's so soft," she marveled.

"Not what a man likes to hear, love," Kage said with laughter in his voice.

"Oh, I meant your skin, not…oh." She blushed furiously as she realized what he meant.

"I know, but he wants to be thought of as turgid, massive, rock hard…anything like that," Kage said. He grasped her hand, stopping her from stroking. "Though it kills me to say this, if you keep doing that, I won't make it inside of you."

Sayah blushed, suddenly nervous. "Kage, there's something I need to tell you," she said. "I haven't…"

He pressed his lips to her forehead gently. "It's okay. We can go as fast or as slow as you want, and if you want to stop, we will."

He kissed her again, then dipped his mouth to her breasts, flicking her nipples with his tongue before suckling deeply, pulling a moan from her throat. She squirmed beneath him, and he dipped a finger between her legs, tracing it slowly across the apex of her thighs. "You're so wet," he said, dipping his finger inside her. "You're more than ready for me."

She arched up against him as he slid down her body, dragging his lips across her skin. A small sound erupted from her throat, reverberating through his chest as he licked and nipped at her sensitive skin. He toyed with the delicate bundle of nerves at her core, setting a pace that had her heart racing.

She hovered on the brink of release, her panting breaths coming faster and faster as he lapped at her, stroking her most intimate areas with his tongue. He felt her tip over the edge and suckled her, relishing the cries of release that filled the silence around them. He stroked her gently with his fingers, soothing her, and kissed her slowly as he slid carefully inside her.

Oh gods, he thought. *She's so–* He breathed deeply, struggling to slow down his movements as he filled her, bursting past her virginity. She sucked in a breath, the quick, sharp pain of his intrusion shooting through her, and stilled completely beneath him. He paused, letting her adjust to the feel of him, until he felt her begin to relax. He thrust deeper, feeling her clench around him. A smile curved his lips as he leaned forward, kissing her deeply, then found a rhythm that exhilarated both of them.

CHAPTER TWENTY-FOUR

Maddox and Reisu stumbled through the servants' entrance of the brothel just before dawn, stinking of liquor and blood. Reisu licked the corner of her lips, wiping away the last traces of rich Cabernet and blood from the fistfight they had enjoyed behind a nondescript tavern in the merchant district.

"You were brilliant," Maddox said, cracking his knuckles. "I've never seen a man cry for mercy quite like that."

"Your father has taught me many things." Reisu shifted out of her fully corporeal form, blurring into a shimmering collection of wisps and smoke. "But my favorite lessons were about the best places to strike to cause a man to beg for release."

"You are truly terrifying," Maddox said with appreciation in his voice. "If you were still in your corporeal form, the things I would do to you…" he trailed off, his eyes shining with lust as they traced over the wisps that formed her curved derriere.

"Oh? And what, exactly, would you do, Maddox?" Dal'gon asked.

Reisu and Maddox jumped, startled, then ran to Dal'gon.

"How was she?" Maddox asked. "We haven't seen you in hours."

"You know perfectly well what happened, flea. This ingrate," Dal'gon gestured to Reisu, "was asked to be hidden in the room, watching everything and ensuring that nothing went awry. Instead, she remained hidden and watched Kage take the girl from me. She watched your brother make a fool of me again, just to take that halfbreed slut out of here and back to their little hideout."

"I—" Reisu stopped abruptly as Dal'gon raised his hand.

"Silence." Dal'gon interrupted, seething. "You allowed him to steal her from me, despite knowing that I want her. Why?"

Reisu opened her mouth to speak, but Dal'gon placed his hand over her mouth and cut her off again. "I don't want to know. I don't care what your reasons were. You are going to fix this. You and Maddox are going to find her and bring her back to me."

"Father," Maddox said. "How are we supposed to find them? They'll undoubtedly have found somewhere else to hide out by now. It's been what? Four hours since this happened?"

Reisu winced as Dal'gon lashed out and struck Maddox across the face, sending blood and spittle flying from his mouth. He shrank back as Dal'gon raised his hand again, but Reisu grabbed him by the wrist and yanked his arm backward. She twisted it behind him, pinning him in place.

"No," she said. "I watched what you did to that girl before Kage intervened. You are done striking people for the night."

"I wouldn't have expected so much insolence from you," Dal'gon said. "After I brought you to this life and made you what you are, I would expect much more humility and kindness where I'm concerned."

"You expect a servant," Reisu said. "Someone to blindly obey your every whim, to entertain you in bed when the others begin to bore you. Your maid, your housekeeper, your madam, your butler, your whore."

Dal'gon said nothing in response, his arm pinned behind his back in her vice-like grip. Maddox stared at the tableau before him, confusion painted across his chiseled features.

"You made me what I am and brought me to this life. But you do not own me, Dal'gon. Do not make me teach you that again." She spat the words at him, blood in her eyes. "You took me from my family and turned me into this. You let me work at your side, but I will not follow you blindly any longer. I expect to be treated as an equal in all of our endeavors moving forward, and I will not be kept in the dark again."

"Reisu," Maddox said. "Let Father go. You've made your point."

Reisu glared at him, but she released Dal'gon's arm. He rubbed his aching wrist and shoulder and looked between his son and majordomo.

"I'll deal with you later, Reisu, when you report to my chambers to debrief regarding this incident. Now, Maddox. When did you start betraying me?" he asked, his voice tight with anger and jealousy.

"I haven't," Maddox said. "You'll notice I'm the one who is here, while Kage is gods know where with the girl."

"And yet, you've put your hands on my *majordomo*," Dal'gon said.

"More than my hands, but that's beside the point." Maddox smirked as he took a step back from his father. "And that isn't betrayal. As she so eloquently told you, she makes her own decisions."

Reisu walked to Maddox and shifted back into her fully corporeal form, wrapping herself around him. She stroked her long fingers down the front of his breeches as she licked the shell of his ear. She smiled as he swelled beneath her hand and cupped him, stroking him through the fabric. Dal'gon glared at them, anger bringing unholy fire to his eyes.

"You would dare—"

"Yes, we dare. Almost every day, sometimes three or four times. You may use me on occasion, but I give myself to your son freely, whenever we both desire it." Reisu kissed Maddox full on the mouth, keeping her eyes open and watching Dal'-gon's rage explode across his face as she swept her tongue into Maddox's mouth. Breaking the kiss, she said, "Now, if you have anything else to say, I would be very polite. As you can tell, I'm not in the mood to be trifled with, and your follies regarding the girl have sorely pressed our luck with concealing your presence here."

"Without the girl, what is the purpose of my presence?" Dal'gon asked. "I followed her mother's lineage here, searching for the child that was my destiny. She is the one I was meant to mate with. I found her, and we can't seem to capture her without my idiotic youngest son getting in the way."

"It sounds like we need to come up with a plan," Maddox said as Reisu continued to stroke him. He bit his lip. "One that will allow us to neutralize Kage and capture the girl for good."

"Suggestions?" Dal'gon asked.

Maddox dressed quickly and slipped through the door, heading out into the night. He wrapped himself in shadows and moved into the alley behind the brothel. Darkness surrounded him. The air stilled as he sat, waiting for the tell-tale creak of the side door.

"What took you so long?" asked a voice from the darkness.

Maddox jumped, whipping his head around. Kage stood behind him, close enough to reach out and touch him.

"What—how—why are you here?"

"That was very eloquent of you, big brother. There can be no doubt that I'm the smart one of the two of us. I'm here to ask for your help."

"What makes you think I would be willing to help you, especially after that comment?"

"I saw your face at dinner, Maddox. I know you don't like what Father is doing to Sayah," Kage said. "And I know about you and Reisu."

"You…what?"

"I know about you and Reisu. The hunting, the secret rendezvous when Father is out, the even more secret ones when he's home…I've seen the way she looks at you, and I've seen you creeping from her bedroom in the dark hours just before dawn." Kage shrugged. "I have no idea how you managed to hide it for so long."

"What are you trying to say?" Maddox asked.

"I'm saying that you can never have her as long as she belongs to Father, and he will never let her go if he knows you want her. So help me defeat him and we can both win."

"I have her whenever I wish as it is," Maddox said snidely. "But yes, I agree that something has to be done about Father."

Kage's head whipped around as he heard the creak of hinges.

"Maddox?" Reisu said in a voice just above a whisper. "Are you here?"

Maddox released the shadows and showed himself to her, and Kage stepped forward into the pale candlelight shining from the candle Reisu carried with her. The dull finish of the pewter holder appeared matte in the dim half-light outside the brothel..

"Kage? What are you doing here?" she asked.

"Come on, Reisu, let's walk and we can discuss everything." Maddox grabbed her hand and snuffed the candle, wrapping them all in shadows.

CHAPTER TWENTY-FIVE

S ayah hid in the alley behind The Rusty Pig, surrounded by the warm comfort of the shadows and darkness. *Where is he?* She thought. *He should have gotten back by now, this is taking too long. He must have been caught, or Maddox refused to help him.* She leaned back against the wall, resting her head against the cold stones. She took several deep breaths, trying to steady herself. *It's okay. He will come back. It will be okay.*

The sound of the crowd at the Pig soothed her, the familiar shouts for ale and voices cracking jokes reminding her of those few happy days with Kage in the suite of rooms above the tavern. She closed her eyes and remembered the sweetness of their first kiss and the soft touch of his lips on hers, and the thought brought a smile to her face.

"Penny for your thoughts?" Kage said from the shadows beside her, startling her from her reverie.

Sayah launched herself at him, wrapping herself around him. She kissed him passionately, diving her hands into his hair, lost in the moment and scrambling to get closer to him, until she heard a woman's quiet, amused chuckle behind her.

"No," she said, letting go of him and backing away. "No. You didn't… you told them where to find me?"

"It's not what you think, Sayah. I swear," Kage said as Reisu and Maddox stepped into the alley. "They're on our side."

"He's gone too far," Maddox said. "This whole thing has gone too far."

"What do you mean?" Sayah asked, staring at them in confusion. "How is this too far? Especially after what he had you do to my parents."

"Let's find somewhere to sit and talk," Maddox said. "I think it's time for you to know everything that I know."

"We'll have to go somewhere else," Kage said. "Dal'gon knows we were staying here before."

"About that," Reisu said. "We actually discussed a plan with him to help him find you and the consensus was that there would be no need to check here because you wouldn't have come back. So we can be safe here for a few hours, at least, which is long enough to discuss everything in detail."

Sayah walked through the alley to the other side of The Rusty Pig and knocked three times in rapid succession on the side door off the kitchen.

"Sayah?" Bess asked from behind the door. "Is that you?"

"Yes, it's me," Sayah said. She smiled when Bess opened the door a crack and peered through. "We need somewhere safe to chat for a while. Are the rooms upstairs still in our name?"

"Yeah, but I haven't gotten the chance to clean up some of the mess up there yet. Kage's brother left one hell of a mess, between the torn sheets and the blood all over the floor."

"That's fine. We'll head up to the sitting room, at least, and get out of your hair." Sayah hugged her friend tight, then kissed her cheek. "And Maddox can clean up his own mess while he's upstairs. Thank you. For everything." She motioned for the others to follow her up the narrow stairs off the kitchen.

"I'll send up a tea service," Bess said, raising an eyebrow at Maddox and Reisu as they passed through the door.

Once everyone was inside and had seated themselves around the table in the private sitting room of their suite, Bess brought up the tea tray, laden with pastries and two pots of well-steeped oolong tea. Sayah poured a cup for herself and leaned back in her chair at the head of the table. "Okay," she said. "Tell me everything."

Kage reached out to grasp her hand. "Maddox, why don't you start from the beginning?"

Maddox looked between them and cleared his throat. "You know that I'm Dal'gon's first child, but nobody is really sure of my exact age. Not even me. Not even Dal'gon, at this point. My mother was a princess in the eastern isles, said to be blessed with magical abilities that let her predict the future." He paused, drawing in a deep breath. "I don't remember much about her, except the faint smell of lilies that dances around the edge of my mind whenever I think of her. The records of her that I could find in the library don't have definitive dates; they read more as treasured legends than histories. They say that she had dark hair and gray eyes, and that she was a fair and just ruler until she went mad after the disappearance of her lover, a prince from another realm."

He sighed, wringing his hands together before continuing. "There was no prince, only Dal'gon. And the madness that took her was his fault entirely. It was the result of his experiments on her. He melded shadow and darkness into her womb during her pregnancy. After I was born, he fled with me and she went mad from the loss and the shadow energy that swelled inside her. Dal'gon is, and has always been, obsessed with breeding the perfect heir." He shook his head, taking a deep breath. "One who would be capable of dominating realms and ruling through deceit and manipulation. A shadow ruler who could topple kingdoms with a word." Maddox stopped, looking at Sayah. "Would you mind pouring me a cup of tea? This is a long story, and I'm already parched."

Sayah nodded and poured him a cup. "Anything in it?" she asked.

"No, just black," Maddox said.

"Would anyone else like a cup?" Sayah asked as she passed the delicate teacup to him.

Kage and Reisu both shook their heads no, and Sayah gestured for Maddox to continue.

"Okay, where was I? Oh yes, Dal'gon's pursuit of the perfect heir. He began experimenting a few centuries ago, tracking families that had different abilities or bloodlines that contained either angelic or demonic blood. Whenever a female held great potential, he would impregnate them or, if they were already pregnant, weave shadow into their wombs the way he did with my mother. The results were…inconsistent, at best, and his frustration grew.

"About fifty years ago, he heard the story of an angel who had given up immortality to be with her human lover. Local legends said that she saw him as he walked one day, his hair shining bronze in the late afternoon sun. She fell in love with him from afar and would visit him nearly every day as she roamed the city, helping the downtrodden and weak. As they grew to love one another, she visited him in the night and lay with him, eventually becoming pregnant. The gods forced her to choose between her newfound family and her immortality. She chose her lover and child, so she was banished to earth permanently. She and her lover raised their baby girl, who they named Kateryna. The little girl grew up to become your mother." Maddox paused, taking a sip of his tea and allowing Sayah to absorb what he had just told her.

"Her name was Kateryna," she said quietly, staring off into space. "And my grandmother...I didn't know...I mean, obviously I knew that I must have grandparents, but I don't remember them. I don't remember most of the beforetimes."

"I remember you mentioning these 'beforetimes' at Dal'-gon's before. You truly have no memory of them?" Reisu asked.

"Yes, that time of my life is blurry at best. Until recently, I didn't even remember how they died," Sayah said. "I still don't really remember anything significant. Mostly just flashes of little things that come to me at random times."

"Oh, I understand. I had wondered how you could be so sure that Maddox caused your parents' death, though, if that is the case." Reisu looked at Maddox.

"The memory of their death came to me in full after I saw Kage for the first time. I saw it as though I floated outside my own body, and I watched him." Sayah shivered at the memory.

"I know it doesn't mean much, but I wasn't aware of the full story at the time," Maddox said. "Only that we were to save you, according to our orders."

"What happened next?" Sayah asked.

"Dal'gon tracked down all the stories he could about the angel and her lover. He believed, well, I suppose he still believes, that her offspring are the answer to creating his ideal heir. He watched your mother grow, following her through her life until she hit her majority and began searching for someone to spend her life with. I watched as he courted her, trying to get her to fall in love with him, but he was unsuccessful. She met your father, just an apprentice at the time, and fell in love with him. They married, and Dal'gon seethed as he watched them start their life together." Maddox rolled his shoulders back, trying to release the tensions in the muscles. "Sorry, I start to ache after sitting for a while. Anyway... He met Kage's mother, a noblewoman who was rumored to be able to read minds, and successfully seduced her, moving into her manor and acting as the picture perfect, doting husband. When he discovered that Kateryna was pregnant, he blanketed himself in shadows and snuck into their home, hiding in plain sight in their bedchamber for weeks, abandoning his then-pregnant lover without a word."

Banked fires of rage lit in Kage's eyes as he listened to Maddox, but he stayed quiet, beckoning his brother to continue speaking.

"This is where most of the story becomes supposition, because he wouldn't admit to anything when we discussed this with him earlier as we made our plans." Maddox rolled his eyes slightly, looking at Reisu. With her nod of approval, he continued his tale. "He says he watched her for days, waiting for her to be alone long enough for him to meld the shadows into her, but he was never able to get the depth he needed to ensure that you were touched by them. Each time he got close enough to influence your development, a shield sprang up between the shadows and you, protecting you from him. When you were born, he got another chance. He stretched ribbons made from shadow toward you as you exited the birth canal and managed to tap your forehead before a flash of gold light emanated from you and dispelled the shadow." Maddox stood for a moment, pacing to the fire and stretching his back, raising his arms high above his head. He stared into the flames for a moment before returning to the table and taking another sip of his tea.

"He watched your family for years, studying you from

afar to see if he had been successful. As your father worked his way up through the ranks as a shipwright, Dal'gon positioned some of his disciples into the crew and tradesmen who worked with him. There were moments where he thought that he saw something, a glimmer of shadow around you, but he couldn't be sure. When you were eight, he sent me out with Kage to check on you because he was busy hunting down a disciple who had gone rogue on another continent. You saw us, despite the shadows we had woven around us, and waved at Kage." Maddox smiled slightly at the memory of Kage's excitement when Sayah had noticed them. "When I reported it to Father that evening after he returned home, I received my orders: eliminate your parents and retrieve you at all costs. I was placed as a member of the crew on his final voyage so I could be in position to eliminate them upon his return."

Sayah's shoulders shook as she cried quietly, the memory of her parents' death still fresh in her mind. "I wish I didn't remember that part," she whispered.

"I wish I hadn't been involved," Maddox said. "Father never gets his hands dirty. If I wasn't here, your parents may have survived. I didn't know why he wanted you or what he had done, and I didn't question his orders at the time. If I had known…I don't think I would have followed them."

"If I'm understanding you correctly, Father has watched Sayah for her entire life, even before she was born, because he believes her family is the solution. When her mother rejected him, he decided to wait for her to bear a child. In his mind, Sayah is the key to creating the heir he desires—a human who can control governments from the shadows, effectively allowing him to take over the world." Kage looked to Maddox for confirmation. "And when he realized that she did possess both her mother's angelic blood and the ability to manipulate shadows, he ordered you to kill her parents and kidnap her."

"Yes," Maddox said. "I succeeded in eliminating her parents, but she ran and we were unable to track her."

"Why is that?" Sayah asked. "Dal'gon can track anyone who manipulates the shadows. Why can't he track me?"

"Truthfully? I don't know," Maddox said.

"I suspect it has to do with your angelic blood," Reisu said. "We spent many hours trying to figure out the shield that protected you and the golden light that came from you during your birth. We were unable to find any information about it, despite years of research, likely because there are no other records of angels choosing to become earthbound. We were tracking you before by following Kage."

Sayah stood and walked to the window, looking out over the dark city streets. She leaned against the window frame and sighed. "I suppose that makes sense," she said. "My mother glowed when you attacked her."

"She did," Maddox said. "She fought back against my shadows with every scrap of the angelic power she possessed. It wasn't enough."

"I know," Sayah said on a sob. Her body shook with the power of her sobs as she purged all of the tumultuous emotion that filled her.

Kage stood and walked to her, placing a hand on her shoulder. He turned her and gently pulled her against him, stroking her back and soothing her. He murmured to her quietly, meaningless nonsense words to steady her breathing and calm her. Finally, her shoulders stilled and her breathing became more even. She pulled back from him, and he wiped the tears from her cheeks with gentle fingers.

"So what do we do now?" Sayah asked.

"Knowing all of this, knowing what I did...you would still work with me?" Maddox was flummoxed.

Sayah nodded silently. "The best chance I have for safety is to find a way to defeat or banish Dal'gon. You came to us, which means you want the same thing. I just want to know one thing, though, before we fully commit to anything...Why?"

Reisu flushed, the wisps that floated around her turning a rosy pink. "Well, you see," she said, "Maddox and I have always been friendly, and a few years ago we began hunting together."

"Hunting?" Kage asked.

"Yes, we go to various areas and pick fights, which allows Maddox to focus his shadow powers and gives me the chance to get the blood I need to maintain a corporeal form," Reisu said.

"A corporeal form?" Sayah's eyebrows knit together in confusion.

Reisu giggled. "I'm a wraith. My corporeal form was ripped from me years ago during one of Dal'gon's experiments. He made me his majordomo after my transition because it made me immortal, and I felt grateful for his protection of me. He taught me to resubstantiate my body through bloodletting and gave me an opportunity to feel powerful for the first time in my life. I, too, regret blindly following him now."

"So in order for you to be here and touch things... you have to drink blood?"

"Sort of," Reisu said. "I have to release blood from another being and take it into myself in some way. Usually, it flies into my mouth during the fight and that's enough to sustain my form, as needed."

"I see," Sayah said. "So you and Maddox go and fight people together, and that makes you want to defeat Dal'gon?"

"That's not all of it," Maddox said, taking Reisu's hand. "I—"

"Oh," Sayah said. "You love her."

"We began to develop feelings for each other and the relationship progressed. Reisu continued to do Father's bidding, but—"

"But I no longer wish to be his whore when he's bored with the girls at the brothel. I want to be with the man I love, and Dal'gon will never set me free." Reisu smiled across the table at Maddox, who appeared flummoxed by her admission of love. "I want a life of my choosing, not a life of servitude to the demon who ripped my human life away."

Kage and Sayah walked back to the table and sat down across from Reisu and Maddox. Sayah rested her head against Kage's shoulder, exhaustion from the revelations setting in.

"Reisu," Kage said. "You and Maddox know Father better than anyone else. What is his weakness? And how can we use it to bring him down?

Reisu blinked, taken aback by the forwardness of his question. Before she could answer, Maddox spoke up.

"I don't know if he has one. If he does, I suspect it's Sayah."

CHAPTER TWENTY-SIX

"What?" Kage shouted, standing abruptly and slamming his palms into the tabletop.

"Shh," Sayah said. "We don't want to attract any attention from downstairs."

"I'm sorry," Kage said. "Maddox just told us that he thinks you might be Father's weakness. How am I supposed to react?"

"I don't know," Sayah said, "but yelling isn't going to help anything, and we don't know who Dal'gon might have working for him."

Kage nodded, his face chagrined.

"Maddox may be right," Reisu said. "His focus on finding the perfect mate to breed his heir has been all-consuming for centuries. Sayah may be the key to defeating him."

"Okay, if that's the case, how is she the key?" Kage asked.

"Nobody knows the true impact of angelic blood on a demon," Maddox said. "It is possible that Sayah's bloodline from her grandmother, plus her ability to wield shadows, could allow her to get close enough to him to strike."

"Strike with what?" Sayah asked.

Reisu looked at her solemnly. "There is only one weapon that is rumored to truly defeat a demon," she said. "A dagger that can only be wielded by one it judges worthy, according to the stories."

"From the look on your face, I'm not going to like what it is."

"You. Only an angel can truly defeat a demon, and the dagger would most assuredly judge you worthy because of your angelic lineage. Over your life, you've cultivated your ability to move within the shadows, and they call to you because of what Dal'gon did when you were a newborn. Now we must find a way to develop your natural angelic abilities so that you can use them against him." Reisu grasped Sayah's hand, squeezing.

Sayah stared at them, mouth agape. "I don't understand."

"You carry the blood of angels in your veins," Kage said. "Because of that, you have some abilities. We don't know what they are because they were never nurtured the way your shadow powers were, but Reisu thinks there is a way."

"Angelic powers are all based around helping others," Reisu said. "I suspect, based on watching you and who your mother was, that you have some sort of telekinetic ability, as well as the ability to make yourself invulnerable." She paused, studying Sayah's face closely. "When Dal'gon was hitting you, what did you feel?"

Sayah flinched. "The force of his hand, the pain of the impact, my blood as it ran down my chin. Why?"

"The wounds you received should have caused far worse damage, maybe even a severe concussion. I was watching as he struck you. Your skin glowed right before the blow, as though you were protecting yourself."

Kage nodded, affirming what Reisu said. "It's true. I

didn't think much of it at the time, but when Reisu mentioned it, I remembered what you told me about your mother during the attack."

"And you believe, all three of you do, that I can somehow learn these powers, despite the fact that we have no idea what they actually are. In a short period of time. Weeks."

"Probably more like days, but yes. We think you can do it," Kage said.

"Days?" Sayah scoffed. "As though that's even feasible. It took me years to figure out how to use the shadows fully."

"With Dal'gon hunting us, we don't have the luxury of time, Sayah."

"Exactly. All the more reason why this should absolutely not be the plan," Sayah seethed. "Even if I wanted to, I couldn't. I'm not—"

"I have an idea," Maddox said, interrupting her rant. He struck out with a whip of shadow, launching it toward Sayah's face.

Sayah held her hand up, blocking her face and waiting for the blow. It never came. She looked up in shock, studying the shadowy tendril that hovered in the air a few inches from her face, suspended in motion. A golden shield surrounded her, shifting and pulsing with light.

"I knew it," Maddox exclaimed. "You can make yourself invulnerable unconsciously. So we just need to figure out the telekinesis."

Sayah sat down heavily, rubbing her forehead with her hand. "Telekinesis is what again?"

"The ability to move things with your mind." Reisu stared at Sayah, focusing intently. "I'm almost positive that you have that ability, too. It's latent in your blood."

"How would you know that?" Sayah asked.

"I don't, not for sure, but it is considered to be a common

ability according to the books I've read while I was researching your family."

"Okay, so what do we do?" Kage asked, squeezing Sayah's hand.

"Sayah, focus on the scone on the plate beside your cup," Reisu said. "Picture it in great detail in your mind. Nothing exists but the scone, each detail and marking becoming clearer as you focus. You can see it shifting, moving toward the bowl to the left of you."

Sayah stared at the citrus scone, inspecting its delicate crumb and the zest and sanding sugar that covered the top of it. She tried to clear her mind, focusing on the most minute details she could think of. *The sanding sugar gleams faintly in the firelight, almost like glitter. The lemon and orange zest are small spots of bright color on the beige biscuit, which crumbles slightly where it first impacted the plate—* "This is bullshit," she said. "I will never be able to do this."

"Focus."

Sayah narrowed her eyes, trying to keep her focus to the scone as her mind raced. Doubts plagued her thoughts as she stared. She pictured it moving with her mind, shifting to the side.

"It moved," Kage exclaimed, leaping to his feet and startling Sayah. "It twitched to the left."

Reisu squealed and grabbed Maddox. He spun her around in excitement.

Sayah frowned slightly, despite their excitement. "But how is me being able to make a scone shift on a plate going to help us in any way?"

"So here's my idea," Maddox said. "You're able to shield yourself from his attacks, preventing him from touching you. This means he can't restrain you to keep you from hitting him with anything. If you stab him through the heart, he won't be able to stop you."

"Stab him with what, though?" Kage asked. "This mystical dagger you were telling us about? How do we know it truly exists and where to find it?"

"There is a dagger," Reisu said firmly. "The blade you hunted down for him. The one you found the night you saw Sayah. He keeps it locked in his desk. It is said that the Dagger of Souls was imbued by the gods with the power to slay demons and defeat evil."

"And he keeps it locked in his desk?" Sayah's voice was incredulous. "Why would he keep something locked in his desk that could kill him?"

"Because it's in an environment he controls, he knows where it is, and no one else has access to it. Nobody even knows where he keeps the key," Maddox said.

"Actually…" Reisu's voice trailed off as a secretive smile lifted the corners of her mouth.

"You know where the key is?" Maddox sounded flummoxed.

"I do."

Silence filled the room as everyone stared at Reisu in shock.

"You know where the key is?" Maddox repeated.

"Yes," Reisu said.

"How? Father never lets anything like that out of his sight, and he never goes into any secure areas of the house if someone else is present to see it."

"Unless…" Kage trailed off.

"Unless I was hidden," Reisu said baldly. She smiled at Kage, returning his amused grin. "As wisps of smoke amongst those from the fireplace. In plain sight, but unnoticeable. Much how I hid myself when you saved Sayah, Kage."

"But you said he knew about that," Maddox said. "He knew you were there, and he saw you after Kage took Sayah."

"He had ordered me to be there. I intentionally hid away from where he instructed me to be and didn't give him our usual signal to show that I was present. He had no way of knowing for sure if I was there. He discovered my presence not from where I was hidden, but from how I left," she said. She hung her head in chagrin. "I returned to my corporeal form and stepped over him as I left the room, rather than floating away in the shadows. I was livid enough that I didn't check, even though I thought he was unconscious. He must have seen me."

"That makes a lot more sense." Kage reached a hand out to Sayah, who grasped it tightly. "So you know where the key is. How do we get it?"

"This is where it gets dicey," Reisu said.

"Why do I get the feeling we will really not like what you're about to say?" Sayah asked, her hand clasped in Kage's.

"We'll have to let Dal'gon capture you and Sayah."

Kage squeezed Sayah's fingers tight as he stared at his brother and Reisu. "No."

"It's the only way, Kage," Sayah said.

"It really is. If Maddox and I bring you in, we'll have to separate you. Kage, we'll put you in Dal'gon's office alone and conveniently forget to bind you. This will leave you free to move around the room and you'll be able to retrieve the key and the dagger. We'll put Sayah in your old bedroom, which is one floor up and four doors down from the office. Do you remember the passage between the two rooms?" Reisu asked.

Maddox grinned. "I had forgotten about that secret passage."

"I haven't thought about it in years. I remember where it is, and I don't believe it was ever boarded up."

"You'll go from the office to your old bedroom. Sayah, you'll be bound loosely to a chair. Kage will help you slip free from the bindings and release you when he gets there. Once he gives you the dagger, he'll hide himself and make sure he's close enough to step in if Dal'gon gets out of hand before you're able to throw up your shield." Reisu paced in front of the fireplace.

"You'll need to hide the dagger somewhere close enough for you to pull it to you, but out of sight so that he doesn't see or sense it. We'll be there with Dal'gon when he comes in for support, as well," Maddox said.

"Okay," Sayah said. "How are we going to get us into the brothel without him knowing?"

"There's no way for us to get in without Dal'gon finding out. We'll bring you in, make sure he's aware that we caught you and tell him that his plan worked. Once we get you into the rooms, we'll go find him and bring him to Sayah." Maddox looked at Kage. "I know you don't want to put her in Father's clutches again, but it's the only way."

"It's not really my decision to make, but you're right. I absolutely don't want to do this." Kage stood and wrapped his arms around Sayah, dropping a kiss on the top of her head. "Are you sure you're okay with this?" he asked her.

"They're right, Kage. It's the only way," Sayah said, tilting her head back to look up at him. "I don't like it. At all. But they are right. The one thing I can't figure out, though, is how telekinesis will help us in any way."

"You won't be able to hold the dagger when Dal'gon

enters the room; he'll expect you to be bound. You'll have to hide the dagger quickly, then return to the chair we bound you to and slip the bindings back into place. When it's time, once you've shielded yourself and have an opening, you'll use your telekinetic powers to bring the dagger to you and stab him. It will have to be through the heart. There's no other option." Reisu looked at Sayah and Kage, still locked in an embrace. "There is always a chance this won't work," she said softly. "But the only way any of us will ever be free is if we try."

"Let's get started, then," Sayah said.

"No," Kage said. "Dal'gon will notice if Maddox and Reisu are gone much longer, and he knows about their relationship now. He'll be paying closer attention. They'll need to leave now and arrive at different times to mask their movements."

"I'll slip out in the afternoon tomorrow," Maddox said, "and come here to work with you. Reisu will come by in the evening for an hour or two before we go hunting. We won't make our move until you're confident that you can move an object to you without hesitation."

"Good night," Reisu said. "I hope you'll both rest well."

"Be safe," Kage said.

"See you tomorrow." Sayah leaned her forehead against Kage's chest, feeling the steady rhythm of his heartbeat. She sighed, leaning closer to feel the comfort of his warmth.

As Maddox and Reisu slipped out the door and down the back staircase, Kage gently cupped Sayah's chin and lifted her face. Kissing her softly, he slid his hand into her hair, reveling in the softness of her curls.

"Let's go to bed," he said. "We could both use some sleep."

CHAPTER TWENTY-SEVEN

Sayah woke as the sky shifted, brightening to the pale pinks and periwinkles of sunrise. She rolled onto her side and looked at Kage, enjoying the peaceful expression on his face as he slept. His lashes shadowed against his cheeks and his chiseled features softened, becoming almost boyish in their relaxed state. Her heart fluttered, and she leaned forward, placing a light kiss on his lips. He sighed quietly, parting his lips and deepening the kiss. He pulled her body closer to his and let his lips drift down her neck to her shoulder. She giggled and nipped his neck, then grabbed the sheets and pulled them over their heads.

Kage let out a huge belly laugh and swatted the sheet back down, wrapping it around them both. "I love you," he said, kissing her.

"I love you too," Sayah said. She curled against him, laying her head against his shoulder. Her stomach growled and she giggled again. "What do you want for breakfast?"

"You," he said, rolling her onto her back.

She started to giggle, but quickly stopped as his lips drifted down her abdomen.

~

The sun was nearly at its peak by the time they left their bed. They giggled like schoolchildren as Sayah wrapped the sheet around herself like a dress and went to the small breakfast table beside the sitting room fire. At some point as they slept, curled around one another in their post-coital haze, Bess had sent up a tray of scones and fruit, with a full teapot steaming beside it on the table. Sayah spread clotted cream over a scone and handed it to Kage as he threw himself into the chair across from her.

"Thank you," he said. He moaned in delight as the delicate scone and clotted cream touched his tongue. "Bess really is a magician with pastries."

Sayah smiled, taking another bite of her own scone. "She is. And you're welcome."

Kage smiled at her, then affected a lecherous leer as he studied her tousled hair and rosy cheeks. "As fetching as you look wearing just a sheet, you should probably get dressed before Maddox gets here."

Sayah laughed, wrapping the sheet more tightly around her breasts. "Oh? You don't want your brother to see me like this?" she asked, batting her eyelashes at him flirtily. "Did you forget that he kidnapped me in my chemise, corset, and bloomers when we were—"

"Don't remind me," Kage said.

"Do you mind helping me with my corset?" Sayah asked as she finished her scone. "Or do you intend to have another scone or two while I get dressed?"

"It's my pleasure to serve, my lady." He stood and bowed to her, grasping her hand and helping her from her chair. "Shall we?"

"We shall," she said with laughter in her voice.

A knock on the door came a few minutes later, and Bess poked her head into the sitting room. "Sayah," she called out, "that gentleman from yesterday is here to see you and Kage."

"Thanks Bess," Kage said as he walked into the sitting room. "Please send him in. Could you help Sayah with her corset? It turns out I'm more adept at removing them than putting them back on."

Bess smirked at him, but nodded her agreement. "I'll have her ready in just a moment," she said.

Maddox came into the room as Bess went to Sayah. He wandered to the table and grabbed a scone, spooning a bit of lemon curd onto it before taking a large bite. "Ommfph," he mumbled before swallowing. "This is incredible."

"Bess is a genius in the kitchen," Kage said. "Just wait until you try her beef pie. It's Sayah's favorite."

"Beef pie? Sounds great. Where is Sayah?"

"Still getting dressed. Bess is coming back up to help her finish dressing and do her hair."

"Hopefully quickly. We have much to discuss," Maddox said with a serious look on his face.

Sayah walked into the room straightening her skirts. "Oh, Maddox. Hi," she said.

"Hi Sayah."

"You look very serious today," she said. "What happened?"

"Sit down and let's talk. Everything is fine," Maddox said. He motioned for Sayah to sit on the settee beside Kage. "When I returned to the brothel last night, Dal'gon was waiting for me."

Sayah's eyebrows knit together with concern, but Maddox held his hand up. "No, no, I promise everything is fine. He assumed I had gone out with Reisu, so he was surprised to see me return alone. I told him I had been out hunting for you to make amends for failing to stop Kage from taking you. I let him believe I was tracing leads that led me into the servants' quarters at the Lyceum. He is anticipating sending me out again tonight to search. I should be able to buy us a few extra days, maybe a week, by spreading out my search radius and following different leads."

"Oh, that is good news," Sayah said.

"Definitely positive. That should give us a little more time to work on Sayah's telekinesis and develop those powers as much as we can."

Maddox nodded in agreement. "And it means I get the privilege of coming here more for the next few days and nights, which means I can continue stealing some of these incredible scones."

"You probably shouldn't come here every night," Kage said. "If Father has you followed…"

"True," Maddox said, a disappointed frown on his face. "But we could find a spot for you to leave me some scones, and I can leave you information?"

"That could work," Sayah said. "There is a ship in the dry dock right now, in for repairs. They haven't started yet. We can use its galley as our dead drop location."

"That's a great idea. Can you tell Reisu when she comes by tonight? I won't see her before she leaves. Father has her practically chained to her desk today with all the work he's given her and told her that he plans to have her 'entertain him' later this evening."

"Of course," Kage said.

Maddox stood to leave. "I'll be back tomorrow, and Reisu will be here later tonight, after she finishes with Father. I'll see you tomorrow, brother." He snagged the last two scones from the tray and gave them a small salute as he took his leave.

CHAPTER TWENTY-EIGHT

Reisu stalked through the halls of the brothel, anger written across the delicate features of her face and flashing in her obsidian eyes. She slammed open the door to Dal'gon's office, storming in and brandishing the ledger she carried before her like a sword.

"What have you done?" she demanded. The fire in the hearth snapped with the surge of power she released, throwing the book at Dal'gon and flipping to the offending entry. "Three of the girls, written off as pensioned, but no funds presented to them. No trace of them anywhere in the house, and no one saw them leave."

Dal'gon smiled at her. "I see that you've decided that you'll work for me, after all," he said sardonically. "What do you care about three girls in a brothel filled with more than thirty?"

"Dammit, Dal'gon, those are my girls. I'm the one responsible for their care and upkeep, I'm the one who makes sure they have what they need. What did you do to them?"

"Just a bit of sport, maybe a little hunting while I'm at it," he said. "Unfortunately, they won't be returning to this plane anytime soon. I suspect they are too disoriented to find their way back."

"You left them in the shadow realm?" She flung the ledger across the room, where it landed on one of the leather club chairs beside his desk. "You took three of my girls to the shadow realm for sport, then left them there. To what end, Dal'gon?"

"It's so enjoyable when they squeal and shriek as I chase them, and the screams when they realize that I'm not the worst thing in that realm...delicious." He licked his lips, the flames in his irises glowing.

Disgusting, Reisu thought. She focused on keeping her face straight and calm, staring him down. "You hunted them, and you decided to let the creatures you permit to roam your realm hunt them too. Then you left them there. Alone?"

"There wasn't much of them left, if that's what you're asking. Just a few scraps the fades will have finished off by now."

"Don't—"

"Don't finish that thought, Reisu," Dal'gon said with an edge to his voice. "You are nothing. Do you forget that I own this place, and those girls, and you? I can do as I please, regardless of who I allow to be responsible for their welfare."

Reisu picked up the ledger. "Fine," she said. "In the future, I ask that you please avoid using our most popular girls for sport as it causes a significant increase in our over-head costs when we have to replace them and train the new ones. I'll be in my office if you need me. I have to finish balancing the books before I can go out hunting later."

"I expect you to assist Maddox in locating the girl. I need to have her before Kage has a chance to put a brat in her belly. I can't have my chance at creating the perfect heir spoiled by that little ingrate," Dal'gon said.

"Yes, sir." Reisu turned and walked from the office, clutching the ledger to her chest. *I hate you,* she thought as she entered the hallway. *I hope he's already succeeded, if only so that you experience the same frustration you've always caused him.*

Reisu's ears perked up at a soft sound from the hallway, her whole body instantly on high alert. The floorboards outside her door creaked quietly, but she heard the near silent footfalls as someone approached her room. The door slid open, the recently oiled hinges quiet, and a shadowy figure slipped inside. He closed the door carefully, barely making a noise as the latch caught and held the door shut.

"Reisu," Maddox whispered in the darkness, his deep voice thick with passion and exhaustion.

"Maddox, you shouldn't be here," she said. "He'll know."

"I don't care, I had to see you," Maddox said. He crossed the room and slipped into her bed beside her. Her skin was smooth against his, but cool, as though she had been out in the night air for too long without a shawl to provide her with warmth. He pulled her back against him and kissed her shoulder, nuzzling his face into her neck. "How did it go with Sayah?"

"She picked up the spoon. She wasn't able to get it to go into the cup, but she picked it up. I'll take that as a win." Reisu snuggled closer to him, enjoying his warmth against her. "Mmm, you feel so good."

"Probably because you're freezing," Maddox said. "You really need to remember to light a fire at night, it's as cold as a morgue in here. But I agree, that is a win. Especially since we only need her to bring the dagger to herself, not do anything with it."

"We'll be working on bringing the spoon to her hand tomorrow. Do you think you'll have time to run through it, too?" She rolled to her side, throwing a leg across him and resting her head on his shoulder.

"Yes, I can try, but most of my day will be spent with Kage, creating a trail of false leads around the city for me to follow. We need to create enough options and sightings that I can track them for days without finding them. That should buy us the time we need to prepare Sayah for the confrontation." Maddox sighed. "If only my day could be spent curled up with you like this instead. I love the way you feel when you're curled against me."

"Maybe one day," Reisu said, tilting her head back to allow Maddox access to her lips for a kiss. "For now, we'll just have to take these moments whenever we can get them."

"Yes, we will." He kissed her shoulder again and ran his hand up and down her arm. "What will we do if she fails?" he asked.

"I don't even want to think about that," Reisu said softly, leaning into his warmth. "But I suppose we'll do what we've been doing all these years. Survive."

"She will succeed. I can feel it," he said. "You should sleep, my love. It was a long day."

"I should, because it really was. Dal'gon took three of the girls into the shadow realm to hunt them. He left them there, Maddox. He left my girls there, said there wasn't much left of them, so he gave them to the fades. Tomorrow will be an even longer day, if I'm right."

"He'll keep escalating until he gets what he wants,"

Maddox said. "We will stop him. We will." He cupped her face in his hand, stroking his thumb down her cheek.

"Good night," she whispered, turning her face to kiss his hand.

"Good night."

CHAPTER TWENTY-NINE

S weat beaded on Sayah's forehead, dripping down her nose before falling to the tabletop. Her eyebrows furrowed to a point, the focus on her face accurately reflecting her mental effort. The spoon sat on the table in front of Reisu, quivering in place. The movement stopped abruptly, and Sayah released an unearthly shriek as she fell forward. Blood trickled from her nose.

"I think it's time for a break." Reisu said. "The stone tombs at Stonehaven weren't built in a day. Developing your abilities is much the same."

"Somehow, I feel as though building those tombs was the easier task," Sayah said, wiping the blood from her face with Kage's handkerchief and taking a sip of water from her glass. The taste of blood filled her mouth as the last vestiges of her nosebleed washed into her mouth. She gagged slightly at the bitter metallic taste. "I'm never going to get the hang of this."

"You will. It'll take practice, and we're trying to force you to make a big developmental leap in a short period of time. This isn't easy, Sayah, but you will get the hang of it." Reisu passed a slice of Bess's dark wheat bread, thick with butter, to Sayah. "We're going to eat now, take a break. You can rest, maybe read a book or take a nap while we pause? When Kage gets back with Maddox, we can try again."

Sayah took a bite of the bread and nodded her agreement. The butter melted on her tongue, a rich, sweet counterpoint to the yeasty crumb of the bread. She devoured the slice, suddenly noticing her hunger for the first time in hours, then reached for the bowl of rich, meaty stew in front of her. "How long have we been working? I feel like I haven't eaten all day."

"About four hours," Reisu said. She leaned back in the chair, the wisps of gray shifting and moving like muscle and sinew. "We won't push you for that long again. I think short spurts might be a better idea, especially since it'll be a short burst that you'll need in order to defeat Dal'gon."

"I understand. Reisu, can I ask you something?" Sayah asked.

"Of course, what would you like to know?"

"If it's too personal, that's okay. I'll understand. Just let me know."

"You can ask me anything, Sayah," Reisu said sincerely.

"The other night, when we were talking and Maddox was telling me everything he had learned, you mentioned that Dal'gon made you this way." Sayah said, unsure of how to continue.

"And you would like to know why I let him?"

"Yes. And how he found you, and…"

"Let's start from the beginning, then," Reisu said. "He found me when I was a child, about two hundred years ago. My parents were exceptional people, known for curing ailments and illnesses that had exceptionally high mortality rates in our village. Their abilities were angelic, but our bloodline was very diluted." She stretched, grabbing a slice of bread and spreading butter across it. She handed the bread to Sayah. "Eat."

"So your family was like mine?" Sayah asked, chewing thoughtfully.

"Yes, but much, much further back. My mother used to say that an angel blessed our family when my great-great-grandfather was alive. I don't know if one of my ancestors was an angel, or just interacted with one; I don't think anyone knew the details."

"So how did Dal'gon find out?"

"I don't know. He was always evasive when I brought it up; he doesn't share any information unless it's necessary or he wants control over a situation and it will benefit him. He took me from my parents when I was thirteen. They had taken me to the market to search for herbs and ointments that we could use for our remedies. Not many things could grow successfully where we lived, and they went through remedies much more quickly due to a wave of serious illnesses that hit the village. We needed to restock, and I desperately wanted to explore the market in a big city after years of being stuck in our tiny village. I don't remember much else about that day, just seeing my parents pulled away from me in the market in Hadrianus. They struck my mother and she fell into the street. Father stopped and tried to help her up. They grabbed him as he reached her and carried them both away." She paused, taking a deep breath to steady herself. "From the moment Dal'gon acquired me, I was an experiment. His disciples grabbed me and brought me here, an entire continent away from where I was raised, and he began performing tests on me immediately. Tearing away bits and pieces of my humanity like they were petals on a daisy," Reisu's eyes filled with tears. "He...I would prefer not to talk about the rest. It is still too painful, even centuries later."

Sayah leaned forward, reaching for Reisu's hand. "I understand. You don't have to tell me about the tests or anything else he did with any details. But I guess what I don't understand is…why did you stay?"

"After the last experiment, the one that failed, when he turned me into this," Reisu said and gestured to herself, making her wisps dance and shift, "I couldn't go home, and very few people were able to see me because I didn't know how to return to corporeal form. I was wisps of pale shadow and a voice, nothing more, and Dal'gon was the only one who seemed to care. He offered me a job running his household, protecting the girls, and I took it because I had nowhere else to go."

"And you stayed because you felt loyal to him for giving you a place to stay?"

"Loyalty was never a part of it," Reisu said, disgust plain on her face. "I stayed because of the girls, Maddox, and Kage. Kage needed me, and Maddox… well, you know how I feel about Maddox."

Sayah chewed a piece of beef from her stew, deep in thought. "Kage needed you?" she asked.

"Yes," Reisu said. "He didn't have his mother, she died during his birth, and Dal'gon is—well, he's Dal'gon. He's a shadow demon; he's not exactly father figure material. Kage was frequently tormented by some of the other disciples because of what his father did to his mother to create him and the messy, tragic way she died, and he needed someone to step in to protect him. To help him."

"So you stayed. You protected him, even though he was the child of the man who ruined you, and you made sure that he had the space he needed to grow into the man he is today. You treated him like your own child because he needed someone to care for him, and you fell in love with Maddox."

Sayah said, summing up everything that Reisu had told her. "But what made you decide to help us?"

Reisu stared at Sayah. "I'm not sure why I didn't expect that question," she said. "I would have asked you the same thing if the situation was reversed." She smiled and patted Sayah's hand. "When Kage was able to overcome Dal'gon to save you, we saw a chink in his armor that gave us an opportunity to set ourselves free. When I told Maddox about what I saw, we knew we had a choice to make—help Dal'gon successfully complete his machinations or defect and help you defeat him. Only one of those options gives us the option to be together, and it's the same option that lets me continue to protect Kage."

"I understand," Sayah said. "Thank you for telling me." She set her spoon into her empty bowl, then looked up at Reisu and smiled. "Is there any more stew?"

Reisu laughed and spooned more stew into Sayah's bowl. "How are you still hungry? You've eaten half the loaf of bread, too."

"I was starving for years. If I hadn't saved Bess when I did, I would probably be dead," Sayah said honestly. "It's almost like I'm eating a lot now to make up for lost time." She tucked into her second helping of stew, a smile on her face.

"Are you ready to get back to work?" Reisu asked.

"Yes, I think so. As soon as I finish this helping." Sayah focused on the spoon in front of Reisu and smiled as it began to shake.

CHAPTER THIRTY

D al'gon paced in front of the fireplace in his bedroom, the light of the flames reflecting on his bare skin. His muscles rippled as he stretched, moving his body around to distract himself from his thoughts. The petite brunette in his bed sat up, pulling the silk sheet with her. She held it to her ample breasts, barely covering her rosy nipples as she stared at him with lust on her face.

"Master?" she whispered. "Can I be of further service?" The rouge on her lips was smeared slightly, but she pouted prettily and batted her eyelashes at him.

"No. Begone." Dal'gon said, his back to her. He tossed a look over his shoulder and glared when he realized she was still in his bed. "Get. Out."

She scurried from the room, as naked as the day she was born. He took no pleasure in the sight of the lash marks from his shadow whip across the bare skin of her back, too frustrated with Kage to enjoy the luscious pain he had inflicted just moments before. Dal'gon slammed shut the door behind her with a wisp of shadow before turning back to the fire. He heaved a sigh and sucked in a deep breath as soon her footsteps disappeared up the spiral staircase, then wrapped shadow around himself and rang for Reisu.

As she entered the room, he released the shadows and stood before her. "Reisu."

"You called for me, sir?" The wisps that made up her body shifted and twisted as she moved toward him, unphased by his nudity and their close proximity. The curve of her waist was accentuated by the v shaped pattern of filigree and vines she had woven into her wisps, angling down between her hips.

Dal'gon's eyes dipped to the point of the v, fire lighting behind them despite his recent release. "Yes. What news do you have for me regarding the search for my idiot son?"

"I haven't seen Maddox today, sir, but my personal search proved fruitless earlier. There were whispers about a beautiful girl with aquamarine eyes in the merchant district, but that's all they were," Reisu said. "Whispers." She shrugged and shook her head. "It seems as though everyone wants the reward we've discreetly mentioned, badly enough to exaggerate or falsify sightings of one or both of them."

"Another day wasted." Dal'gon turned his back to Reisu, staring into the fireplace again. "What else do you know?"

"Not much. The only sighting of Kage was one alley over from here, and there's no way it could be true. They wouldn't be so stupid as to stay close to your home." Reisu stepped closer to the fire, standing beside Dal'gon as they stared into the flames.

"I agree. Check it anyway," Dal'gon said. "Send Maddox to me as soon as he returns. And get some blood in you. I expect you to be fully corporeal when you return to me."

"Yes, sir," Reisu said. She turned to glide out of the room but stopped when a tendril of shadow tangled amongst the wisps of her leg. "Sir?"

"Do not cross me again, Reisu. You are mine." Dal'gon released her and used a breeze made of shadow to push her out the door.

Reisu crept through the halls of the brothel, trailing her wisps along the silken wallpaper as she approached Maddox's room. The sounds of lovemaking and screams of pleasure echoed as she passed the infamous viewing rooms. One of the girls gave her a small curtsy as she exited the luxuriously appointed dungeon known as the whipping chamber. She nodded in response, skirting around the pile of petticoats in the hallway so she could take the spiral staircase up a level to the disciples' quarters. Most of the rooms were empty now, as the vast majority of the disciples were off following Dal'-gon's orders across the globe and in the shadow realm, so she was able to ensure that nobody else would see her as she snuck into his room.

She turned the knob and slipped inside the room. She reached for the vial of blood Maddox kept for her in the top drawer of his bureau, slipping her wisps through the space between the glass and the cork. As she absorbed the essence of the blood and removed her wisps, she felt the strength of its life force enter her, pulsing and strengthening her, allowing her to regain her corporeal form. She crossed the room and pulled the smooth linen sheets back, removing the warming pan and climbing into the bed. She rubbed her cold feet against the warm sheets as she covered herself.

His pillow smells just like him, she thought. *Sage and cedar and something dark and mysterious that I can never manage to place.* She sighed. *I love his scent.* She grabbed the pillow and hugged it to her body, holding onto it while she waited for him to return. She pulled the warm sheets and coverlet over herself, nestling into the feather mattress and luxuriating in the comfort and warmth while she waited.

Sleep found her unexpectedly, her exhaustion from the past days of constant work and anxiety finally catching up to her. She startled awake when the door creaked open just before the sun rose in the sky, bringing the dawn and a new day with it. Maddox walked into the room and divested himself of his muddy riding boots and sack coat before unbuttoning his waistcoat. With a soft groan, he slumped into the chair beside the dying embers of the fire and put his feet up on the worn leather ottoman in front of the chair. He steepled his fingers below his chin and stared into the glowing coals.

"How did it go?" Reisu asked, pulling the sheets with her as she sat up.

"It went well enough," Maddox said. "We laid a false trail into the hidden rooms of the library for you to follow later. There is a small window in one of the rooms that can be accessed from the ground. We left a torn bit of one of Kage's jackets there, and he made sure to add a couple drops of blood so it looks like he cut himself as he crawled inside. And I was able to get into Our Lady of Charity to lay the ground-work for another sighting of Sayah. The priestess there is familiar with her and will claim to have seen her lighting candles late at night."

"How did you get the priestess to agree to help us?" she asked, a disgusted look on her face. "She's usually more interested in what others will do for her than in true charity. You know how they are—greedy from the tops of their heads to the tips of their gold-painted toenails."

"Kage made a significant donation to the collection plate when we arrived," Maddox said, a smirk on his face. "It helps that the priestess badly wants Sayah to become an acolyte. The donation came with the promise that Sayah will consider joining them after she is safe to move about freely again."

"'Consider' being the operative word, of course. That's brilliant," Reisu said. "So everything is moving according to plan. Was she making progress with moving the spoon when you left?"

"She got it to move about an inch and managed to lift it from the table, so there is definitely progress." Maddox stood and stretched, then crossed the room and climbed into the bed beside her. "She said you told her about what Father did to you."

"Not in great detail, at least not with regard to the methods he used when he turned me into this. She didn't need to hear about the bloodletting or the ritual spells, or the sacrifice of one of your brothers as a conduit to increase his magic. She's been through enough of her own pain to deserve a reprieve from that of others. But yes, I told her about being stolen from my family and experimented on, and we talked about the reasons why I stayed."

"Why did you stay, Reisu?" Maddox asked.

"For the girls, to protect them. And for you. And for Kage, to make sure he had someone who would care for and look after him," she said, feeling the weight of the truth lift from her shoulders as she said the words out loud to him for the first time. "I knew I needed to stay to protect Kage, and I knew that I wanted to be with you. Even if I could never truly belong to you because of what your father did to me." She grabbed his hand and held it.

"Reisu." Maddox's voice was filled with passion as he leaned forward and pulled her body against his, using his hands to press her tight against him. He kissed her madly, his lips bruising and his teeth nipping at her bottom lip before his tongue slid into her mouth. "Reisu."

"Yes. Maddox, yes." She purred low in her throat and threaded her fingers through his hair, pressing his mouth even harder against hers. "Please," she begged. She tilted her head back and to the side, allowing him full access to the tender skin of her neck.

Maddox ravished her neck with his lips and teeth, the stubble from his chin and cheeks leaving a reddened trail along her skin. He growled in his throat, pushing her backward onto the bed as he kissed his way across her breasts and abdomen. He flicked his tongue into her belly button lightly, the thin ribbon of control he held over his lust threatening to snap. "Why did you stay, Reisu? Say it."

"Because I love you." She gasped as he slid up her body and kissed her again, intense emotions bubbling within her and threatening to overcome what was left of her self control. She untied his breeches and pushed them down his hips, grasping his buttocks and digging her fingernails into them. "Because I need you desperately, like a human needs water and food to survive. Because I want you, every second of every day."

He pillowed her head with his arm as he slid himself beneath the sheets and pressed against her. His manhood stiffened and flexed against her, pushing toward her center. "I love you," Maddox said, slipping inside her and feeling her stretch as he filled her. "I love you."

"Always," Reisu sighed against his mouth as he took her lips with his.

～

Damon wandered through the alleys beside the brothel, searching for any sign of Kage. Dal'gon was livid, demanding that Kage be found, and all of the disciples who were still in Ship's Haven were sent out in search parties. Rewards far greater than they had ever been offered were in play, with Dal'gon promising everything from hunting in the shadow realm to the whores in his brothel for whichever of his disciples managed to successfully capture Kage.

Even Maddox is out hunting for him, he thought. *I can't believe Dal'gon pulled him from whatever assignment he was on to search for his brother. He never gets assigned grunt work like this; it's always more serious missions. I suppose I should be grateful to even be included, since all the others tell me what a failure I am whenever I return from a mission.* The alleys were cramped, boxes and crates stacked in haphazard piles, and he hid himself behind one such stack, pulling shadows around himself to conceal his presence. *I'm lucky to be alive after the mess I made with that blue eyed girl's father. I thought for sure he'd kill me when we returned without the girl. I shouldn't have taken the money from her father's wallet.*

Across the alley, the petite cook of The Rusty Pig poked her head out the door of the kitchen, looking around before tossing a bucket of scraps out onto the pile of refuse. The smell reached him where he hid, hints of thyme and rosemary, carrots, and brussels sprouts with some sort of cream.

Why is she throwing out perfectly good food? He wondered. He watched her sweep and mop the kitchen, putting a pie in the window to cool and gazing outside. She pushed the sweat-damp curls back from her forehead, closing her eyes for a moment..

She looks lost in thought, he thought to himself. *She sure is pretty. I wonder if Kage and the girl would be stupid enough to come back here. Maddox said the leads were taking him all over the city, as though they were intentionally being seen everywhere.* He sighed. *Or people just want a reward and hope that they can fool us.*

He dozed off watching the kitchen door, not realizing how much time passed as he let himself drift. The sound of crates shifting close to him brought him back to the present, and he stared ahead at the man climbing the stairs.

"Bess," the man said, shrugging his cloak off his shoulders as he walked through the door. His large frame hid the cook and anyone else from view. "Could you have a bath sent up for us? I'm sure Sayah will want to bathe before we—"

Damon stopped listening as he saw Kage's face as he turned back toward the door. *I found them. Not Maddox, not any other disciple. Me. The failure.* He waited until Kage disappeared up through the narrow door that led to the back staircase from the kitchen, then stalked off in the direction of the brothel, eager to share his news with Dal'gon.

In their bedroom above The Rusty Pig, Kage gently pulled a hair brush through Sayah's curls. The rhythmic motion soothed her after the strain of forcing her telekinetic powers for the majority of the day. The headache that had formed behind her eyes had dulled, and the gentle brushing of her hair pushed her closer to relaxation.

"Mmm," she said softly. "That feels amazing."

"Is it helping? I can only imagine that having your hair up with all those pins in it didn't do much to help your headache," Kage said.

"Yes, it's definitely helping. I had forgotten that my head could ache so badly. This hasn't happened in years. But then

—" she stopped. "But then, I never really had a reason to wear my hair up, and I didn't have any pins to hold it there if I did have a reason. If I wanted it out of my face, I braided it or tied it in a knot on the back of my head."

"I'm glad to be able to do this for you, then, now that you do have a reason and the pins to do it." Kage kissed the top of her head and set the hair brush down on the table next to them. "What would you like to do now?" he asked.

"I'm not sure," she said. "Possibly some tea by the fire?"

"I'll run down and ask Bess to send up a tray," Kage said.

"Thank you, love."

As Kage left the room, he turned and winked at her. "Be back in just a moment."

Sayah giggled, then grabbed the hair brush and returned it to the dressing table in the second bedroom of their suite of rooms. Though she hadn't slept there in weeks, she kept her things there and used the room as a dressing room, giving her privacy when she wanted or needed it. She sat on the bed and looked around.

I can't believe everything that has happened, she thought. *My life has been flipped upside down since the day Kage saved me from those street toughs in the alley below us. Everything changed for me when he walked into my life.* She picked up the skirt of her gown, studying the tiny stitching and embroidery that lined the hem. *I never thought I would own something so fine, or be with someone who would want me to have something like this. This is so much more than I ever dared to dream about.*

The door knob turned in the sitting room and she sprang to her feet, rushing out into the room to greet Kage. "Darling, I—"

"We have to go," Kage said. He grabbed a pillow, removing the case, and began stuffing her clothes into it.

"Maddox is on the way with Reisu. Dal'gon had several other disciples tracking me, and one of them saw me yesterday when I got back here after we laid a false trail near Our Lady of Charity. It sounds like he was camped out in the alley between here and the brothel. We have to run now. Maddox saw him entering Dal'gon's office about ten minutes ago."

"Oh gods," Sayah said. "Does Bess know?"

"Yes, I told her when I found Maddox's note tucked into the hearthstones beside the fireplace in the kitchen. We have to leave, Sayah. Now." He stared at her, mouth agape. "Why are you still standing there?"

She narrowed her eyes at him, then looked just over his shoulder. The hair brush flew toward her and landed in her hand. She gasped. "I did it!"

"You did. Now let's get the hell out of here."

"Okay," Sayah said. "Just let me grab my—"

"No. We have to go. Now." Kage grabbed her arm and dragged her down the stairs and out the kitchen door. "Wrap us in shadow," he said.

She obliged, shrouding them in dense, nearly opaque shadow, and they ran toward the main street. They squeezed between the walls of two tenements, ducking into a small alley that angled north between the merchant district and the docks. The sound of church bells rang out, echoing through the rabbit warren surrounding them. Sayah released the shadows and they blended into the throng of people pushing up toward the sanctuary at Our Lady of Charity. The crowd chanted and sang to praise the Lady, and Sayah smiled slightly as she pulled Kage into a different alley straddling the edge of the dock district and the canals.

"Here," she said. She pushed aside a small pallet of wood that concealed a door and went inside. "This has been abandoned for years, so we'll be safe in here." She sat down on an overturned crate and took a deep breath.

"How did you—" Kage started to say. "You've stayed here before."

"Yes," Sayah said. "One particularly bad winter, when I had no way of staying out of the elements other than staying in the sanctuary or hiding here on the days when it was too snowy or cold for me to huddle down in the alleys near one of the inns or taverns. When the head priestess became too pushy about me joining the order and started to move me out of the sanctuary and into the dormitory, I came here to get away from her."

"That makes sense," Kage said. "She's still determined to have you join the order, even after years of you refusing. At least we were close enough to this building that we were able to find our way here and use it as a hideout."

"I'm glad I remembered this place." Sayah reached out to him, and he grabbed her hand. "Kage," she said. "I love you."

"I love you too." He flipped another crate over and sat down beside her, staring at the door. "I wish there was better airflow in here," he said. "It's sweltering."

"It was unseasonably warm today," Sayah said. "It's almost the autumnal equinox, but it felt more like midsummer this afternoon."

Sayah nodded. They sat together quietly for some time before Kage pulled out a deck of cards and began to shuffle mindlessly.

"Want to play?" he asked after a few minutes, the cards flying in an arc between his hands. At her nod, he dealt the cards out and taught her to play War to pass the time.

"This is brilliant," Sayah said as she pulled a card from her hand using her mind, setting it on the stack before them. "I didn't even know you had a deck of cards."

"A man should always carry two things," Kage said. "A deck of cards and a knife. Never know when they'll come in handy."

Sayah laughed quietly. "I can see that. They've both come in handy since I've met you."

"A lot of things have come in handy since we met," Kage said. He leaned over and kissed her softly. "Now, let's get back to the game." He slammed another card down, a wicked grin on his face.

Sayah continued to play, and the two did battle with cards for several hours as the sounds of night began to creep through the boarded up window openings on the building. "Shh," she said, lowering her voice. "Do you hear that?"

"Hear what?" Kage said.

A small crash echoed, overwhelming the gentle lapping of waves at the shore that sounded in the distance and Sayah startled. "That," she whispered. "Something is happening outside." She wrapped herself in shadow and crept to the window, peering between the boards to look outside.

"What do you see?" Kage whispered.

"I think someone is here, but I can't see who. It looks like there are three people outside; two of them appear to be fighting with the other one."

"Dal'gon." Kage's voice sounded like steel. "He's here, he must have followed Maddox and Reisu. It's time for us to move."

"No, I don't think it's him," Sayah said as she peered through the crack in the boards. "They're on the small side. They look like students at the Lyceum. Let's wait and see what happens. If they move toward the door, we'll get out."

Kage nodded stiffly and wrapped his arms around her. They stood at the window, covered in a blanket of shadows, and watched as the two slightly larger people beat down the smaller one before fleeing. As the smaller one limped away, the light of a lantern hanging outside the door of a building across the alley illuminated his face, confirming that Sayah was right—they were students, no more than fourteen years old. Satisfied that they remained hidden for the time being, they moved deeper into the interior of the room and settled down onto the floor. Kage wrapped his jacket around Sayah's shoulders and pulled her to him.

"Try to rest," he said. "I have a feeling that our time is up."

"I will." She leaned her head against his shoulder and nuzzled him. "You should try to rest, too. This won't be easy on either of us."

CHAPTER THIRTY-ONE

D al'gon and Damon stalked through the shadows outside The Rusty Pig, carefully avoiding the pools of light spilling out from the windows, thrown open wide to let in the cool night air. Inside, every gas lamp was lit and the crowd of customers sang along to a rowdy pub song. The kitchen was dim, only embers burning in the hearth.

"Perfect," Dal'gon said as he looked through the open top of the dutch door leading into the kitchen from the alley. "The cook has gone home for the night." He slipped through the shadows outside the door and reached in carefully, picking the lock with tendrils of shadow.

"He went up the back stairs," Damon said, pointing. "Through that door to the left. I'm not sure where their room is, but they must be on the back half of the building, or he would have gone in the front."

Dal'gon smacked him. "Or he went in the back door because he wanted to remain hidden."

"Or that, but I think it's because of where their room is. He was very familiar with the cook," Damon insisted, his cheeks growing ruddy with embarrassment. "I know what I saw, boss."

Dal'gon narrowed his eyes, refusing to concede the point, and they remained completely silent as they slipped the door open and snuck through the door and up the stairs. The old wood creaked as they approached the landing, and Dal'gon stopped, holding his fist up to stop his disciple from moving further forward. They paused for a moment, listening to the raucous noise from the taproom below them; when Dal'gon was satisfied that no one was coming for them, they crept into the hallway and checked each door.

"Empty." Dal'gon seethed. "All empty."

"I don't understand," the disciple said angrily. He cringed back from Dal'gon as he turned to face him. "He was here. I saw him here yesterday."

"Fool. He knows we are hunting him and the girl, so he took advantage of that and tricked you," Dal'gon said, color rising in his cheeks. "He isn't here. There's nothing in any of these rooms." He slammed his fist into the wall and stormed back down the stairs, not bothering to wrap himself in shadows to keep someone from seeing him.

The disciple followed, wrapping shadows around himself and extending them to cover Dal'gon. He stepped carefully down the stairs, avoiding the loose board on the bottom step and dodging around the large worktable in the center of the kitchen. *I'm screwed,* he thought. *I'll be stripped of my powers for this failure. He said this was my last chance to prove myself. I can't fail again.* He focused on keeping them covered by shadow as they fled from The Rusty Pig's kitchens and out into the night.

～

Maddox and Reisu watched as Dal'gon passed them in the alley from their hiding spot. The shadows surrounded him suddenly, and Maddox sensed another disciple in the area as they walked by. "Someone else is with him," Maddox said once they were sure the alley was clear. "I don't know which disciple, but Dal'gon brought someone else along with him tonight."

"They left empty handed, which means that Kage got her out on time. Where is the rendezvous point?" Reisu asked.

"There is an empty house two streets over from Our Lady of Charity. We will meet them there in the morning, unless Kage is able to get a note to our drop point before then."

"Okay," Reisu said. "What are we doing until then?"

"Well, the rooms are already paid for," Maddox said. "But I suspect it would be smarter for me to return and find out what Dal'gon knows."

"I should go back, as well. I can bring back some perfumes and oils for the girls. I have them stashed in the alley, so I can pretend to have been out shopping. I'll bring one of the tavern girls with me as a recruit for the house, as well." She kissed him softly.

"Good idea. You'll go first, then, to give you time to find a tavern girl who is willing to return with you."

"I have a few connections that I've been cultivating," she said as she stood and released her corporeal form, turning to wisps of delicate gray mist. "I'll see you there."

Maddox took a deep breath as Reisu left, then hid himself and crept closer to the back door of The Rusty Pig. He jiggled the handle and waited. The latch released as the knob inside was turned, and he slipped into the door, closing it behind him.

"Well?" he asked.

"He came through," Bess said, wiping cobwebs and dust

from her skirts and hair. The door to the small storage room off the kitchen stood open slightly, streaks of dust wiped away where her skirts had touched. "They checked every room, all empty. I got what was left into the storage room before he got here, and I was able to hide in there without him finding me."

Maddox picked a small spider off of Bess's shoulder and flicked it into the fireplace. "What did you hear?"

"Whoever he had with him saw Kage here yesterday, then told Dal'gon and led him to the Pig. It sounded as though that person decided to just sit in the alley here, rather than actually looking for them. Dal'gon was…displeased when Kage and Sayah weren't here."

"Did you see the other person? What did he look like?" Maddox asked.

"A little shorter than you, fat and scruffy. His beard looked dirty and there were crumbs in it," Bess said. "He seemed unpleasant and didn't have the look of someone with a lot of intellect."

"Thank you," Maddox said. "I appreciate all your help on this."

"You're welcome. Anything to help Sayah. She saved me once. I'm happy to have the opportunity to help her now."

Maddox thanked her again and cloaked himself, drifting out the door and back toward the brothel. He felt the wards go off as he walked through the alley door and released the shadows to greet Dal'gon.

"Father, it's a pleasure to see you," he said. "But you don't look pleased. What happened?"

"I've been off hunting your brother with Damon. He insisted that he saw Kage at The Rusty Pig, despite what you said about having checked the area. I brought him with me to check it out, but all of the guest rooms were completely empty and there was no sign of Kage or the girl anywhere." Dal'gon's voice was matter of fact, but his face betrayed his anger.

"And Damon? What did he have to say for himself when they weren't there?"

"His reasoning was unsatisfactory and unsound. He swears that he wasn't mistaken and that Kage must have spotted him from his hiding spot, despite there being no sightings of them anywhere near that tavern in over a week. He is no longer a concern of ours."

"I see," Maddox said. "The shadow realm?"

Dal'gon nodded slightly, just a faint shift of his chin as he glared out the window at the night sky.

"What now?" Maddox asked.

"Now you'll sit with me and tell me what you found today. Then we shall see." Dal'gon gestured for Maddox to follow him and walked from the foyer.

As they entered Dal'gon's office, Maddox felt the air shift around them. Reisu materialized beside the desk and picked up her ledger. She counted out the vials in her bags and made a few markings in the book, then set everything down on the desk.

"Dal'gon, I—Oh, Maddox is with you. Good." Reisu straightened and shifted into her corporeal form. "I spotted something odd while I was out earlier and wanted to discuss it with both of you, so this will save me time."

"What did you see?" Dal'gon asked, intrigued.

"I thought I saw Sayah as I left the perfumery with the girls' order. When I approached, she vanished into a puff of smoke."

"A puff of smoke?" Maddox asked. He arched a brow at the thought.

"I know, it's very strange. I stopped by the library and

checked a few books to see if I could find anything about this type of phenomenon, but there was nothing. No record of any angel having the ability to disappear that way. The only creatures who can disappear fully are the djinn, and we haven't had one of those in over a millennia, according to the histories."

"A djinn. No, absolutely not," Dal'gon said. "I eradicated those myself several centuries ago. There is no way. But how…" He trailed off. "Unless she has been working to develop skills that she shouldn't be able to use, though I have no idea who would teach her such a thing. What else did you find?"

"Not much," Reisu admitted. "The perfumer didn't recognize either of them when I described them, and I couldn't pick up the trail again. It looks like another false trail."

"I see. My night was also wasted on a false sighting," Dal'gon said. "I require distraction this evening."

"One of the girls, perhaps?" Maddox suggested. "There is a particularly luscious brunette that recently joined the staff. I've heard that she's already among the most popular of our ladies. Or perhaps we could hunt together in the shadow realm?"

"No. None of that will distract me from the issues at hand. Reisu, I shall see you in my chamber in twenty minutes. I have business to discuss with Maddox before you entertain me." Dal'gon held the office door open for Reisu.

"Yes, sir," she said as she passed through the door.

"Now," Dal'gon said as he closed the door behind her. "Let's get down to business. What did you discover while you were out?"

"Not much new," Maddox said. "No sightings of Sayah at all, and only one sighting of Kage that was viable. Someone recognized my drawing of him in the merchant district; he picked up a pair of breeches and a shirt from a tailor near the canal, but the tailor said they were much too small for him. Apparently he said he had a little brother in need of new clothes."

"Breeches?" Dal'gon asked. "Why would he need breeches that are too small?"

"I think they are disguising Sayah as a boy. It explains why we haven't had any legitimate sightings of her, other than Reisu's possible sighting earlier." Maddox sighed. "It's clever, I'll give him that. If they hide her hair and keep her face out of sight as much as possible, no one would recognize her."

"That could be it," Dal'gon said, his mouth downturned in a thoughtful frown. "Is there anything else I need to know?"

"I'll be checking near the Lyceum and the library again tomorrow, then heading up toward Our Lady of Charity. Sayah was spotted there several times before she met up with Kage, according to an acolyte I met in the merchant district. She, the acolyte, said that the head priestess has been desperate for Sayah to join the Order for quite some time, possibly even years. She may go back to what she knows, even at the risk of them forcing her to join the Order."

Dal'gon nodded. "I see," he said dismissively. "There is much to consider tomorrow when we begin our search anew."

"I'll see myself out," Maddox said, sensing the dismissal in Dal'gon's voice. He stood from the armchair, giving his father a terse nod. "I'll come to your office tomorrow evening to let you know what I've found."

In the corner, pale wisps of smoke twisted slightly, shimmering in the light of the flames, then disappeared between the floorboards.

CHAPTER THIRTY-TWO

S ayah slept, curled into the hammock they made out of carefully knotted blankets and ropes they found in a storage closet within the abandoned building. Kage watched her sleep for a few moments as he sat beside her, admiring the soft curve of her lips when she smiled at something in her dreams. He gently stroked her hair and dropped a kiss onto her forehead before he slipped out of the door and into the alley, heading toward the wide street that led to the merchants district and the fruit stands that lined the canal.

She loves oranges, he thought. *Hopefully I can find one, or maybe a pomegranate or persimmon. I wonder if she's tried pomegranate before.* He walked quickly, determined to find something more substantial than stale bread and dried meat for their breakfast.

The carts and stalls of the marketplace along the main canal were just beginning to roll up their canvas coverings when he arrived, propping their awnings on tall poles to provide themselves with some shade in the unseasonably sunny weather. The chatter of friendly voices engulfed him, reminding him why he loved Ship's Haven and chose to stay when Dal'gon offered him the chance to become an operative on another continent. This was home.

"Good morning," the shopkeeper said from beside her basket lined stall as he approached to inspect the variety of exotic fruit at her stand. She pushed a strand of unruly hair back from her forehead, then pushed her sleeves up to her elbows. "How can I help you?"

"I'm looking for oranges and pomegranates," he said. "Something to feed my lady friend when she wakes."

"You've come to the right place for the oranges, but I've not seen pomegranates in some time. Trade with the Turks has damn near come to a stop in the past decade."

"Why is that?" Kage asked as he studied her carefully curated display of fruit.

"Something about a shipwright who was killed. It seems his crew believed it had something to do with the Turks; they had just returned from there. Some sort of curse, I heard. It claimed the man's entire family, even his little girl." She sighed. "You could try further down, near the ships, if you were so inclined; some of them are brave enough to venture into those territories, but they stay close to their ships and crew to protect their investment. Or is there something else you could be looking for?"

Kage picked an orange from the display and palmed it, feeling its firmness before smelling the rind. He handed her the orange, then passed her a silver mark. "Perhaps a persimmon or pastries, if I'm not able to find a pomegranate anywhere," he said as the proprietor handed the orange back to him and gave him his change.

"There is a bakery on the main square, diagonal from here, then across the green, that makes fantastic pastries. If you can't find a pomegranate and are looking for something exotic, I would go there. The shop is Patisserie des Arts, and the chef…she is a true artist."

"Thank you," Kage said. He turned to go, then tossed a glance back over his shoulder.

The shopkeeper smiled at him and turned back to her fruit, adjusting the display to make up for the orange that Kage had just purchased.

Something about her seems very familiar, Kage thought, studying the messy hair and rolled sleeves she wore, to all appearances as proud as any queen would be in her regalia. *I'll have to be more careful when I head back to Sayah, just in case.*

He walked further down the canal and ducked between two stalls, twisting the shadows and concealing himself. He watched for several minutes to ensure he wasn't being followed. He started to leave his hiding spot, having decided to forego any other purchases in favor of returning to Sayah and ensuring her safety. He slid between the stalls and the wall lining the canal, sticking to the shadows and heading back toward their hideout.

Kage stopped suddenly as he got close to the alley where the entrance was hidden, catching a flash of light from inside one of the windows of another abandoned building nearby. He slipped through the shadows and peered into the window, catching a glimpse of a little boy holding a lit candle, his back to the missing panes of glass.

Okay, he thought. *Just a little boy. Not a threat.* He turned back to the entrance of the alley and watched for a few minutes, tracking the shadows to search for movement that any other person wouldn't be able to see. When he was sure that no one else was around, he headed toward the pallet that blocked the door into the abandoned house, shifting it so he could head inside.

Sayah jumped at the sound of the door. "What the hell?" she said. "Where were you?"

Kage released the shadows and held out the orange, smiling at her. "I went to get you some breakfast," he said.

Sayah grinned back, her surprise plain on her face. "You went to get me some breakfast?" She held her hand out for the orange, but he pulled it back from her.

"I remembered that you like oranges, and we don't have Bess to send up fresh scones and fruit for us, so I figured someone had to make sure you eat." He smirked, holding the orange up again. "But if you're mad at me for startling you—"

She pounced on him, kissing him on the cheek with a grin. "Thank you, thank you, thank you," she said as she reached for the orange. "But what will you eat?"

Kage laughed and said, "Some of that orange, obviously. I didn't just pick it up for you. Maybe some of the leftover rye bread and cheese that Bess packed for us when we were fleeing The Rusty Pig."

"Oh, I had forgotten about that. That's a great idea." Sayah dug her fingernails into the skin of the orange, pushing them through the pith and peeling the dimpled flesh away to reveal the sweet wedges of fruit beneath. She divided the orange in half and handed a chunk to Kage, smiling as she popped a piece into her mouth.

"Thank you," he said. He peeled off a slice of the flesh and bit into it, enjoying the sweet burst of juice when his teeth penetrated the flesh. "This is delicious. How did they become your favorite?"

"Oh, I haven't thought about that in years," Sayah said. "Papa used to bring them home for me when he'd sail out with one of his ships."

"It's crazy that he would go out on sea voyages, despite

having a family here. The crew really let him sail with them? Without complaint?" Kage asked.

Sayah nodded, a grin on her face. "Papa liked to see how his designs fared on the water. He was a sailor at heart, and he wanted to be on the water whenever the opportunity existed. One of the few memories I have of the beforetimes is waiting for him to come home, standing in the front window of our house, ecstatic to see what treats he would bring me. He always had something for me; an orange, candy, some small trinket. And a locket for Mama."

"It sounds like he loved you both a whole lot. I'm really sorry, Sayah," Kage said. He took another bite of orange and watched her as she chewed. "That my father took your parents from you. That he has hunted you like a prize deer. You deserve so much better than that and…well, thank you for understanding that I'm not like my father."

"You protected me when you could have kidnapped me right then. You didn't know who I was, but you dragged those men in the opposite direction so that I could get away. I still don't understand why." She peeled a chunk of pith from the last of her orange sections, then divided it into smaller pieces and popped one into her mouth. "But I am grateful," she said as she chewed.

"I didn't know if you were one of Father's disciples or not, and I wasn't going to take the risk that you were. Letting you be hurt would have been seen as a threat to his power, the start of a coup. Then, when I saw you again at the library…" he trailed off and took a deep breath. "I knew I had to take you to Father, but I was drawn to you from the first moment I heard your voice."

"You don't have to say things like that," Sayah said. "I was a street urchin wearing a borrowed dress who hadn't had a real bath in weeks. I'm sure I was repulsive."

"You absolutely weren't repulsive in any way. You were the most beautiful creature I had ever seen. You still are." Kage leaned in and kissed her, tasting the sweet tart flavor of the orange on her lips. "I love you."

"I love you too." Sayah leaned against him and pulled his face down to hers, kissing him again. "What else happened while you were out?"

"Not much. I had intended to do a bit more shopping, but the exotic fruits shopkeeper looked familiar and it worried me after the close call we had yesterday. I ended up strolling down to a gap between market stalls and concealing myself, then sneaking away from the canals to come back here." He paused, considering whether or not he should tell her. "Then…The only other strange thing that happened was a flash of light from one of the buildings a little further down, on the other side of the alley. But when I looked, it was just a little boy, maybe eight, sitting with a candle in another abandoned house across the alley from us."

"Poor kid. I wish that we were in a position to help him. Being on the run isn't the most stable environment for a child." Sayah frowned.

"I know," Kage said. "But one day, we can help as many children as you want."

"Once we defeat Dal'gon."

"Exactly. Once Father is gone, we will have the rest of our lives to help anyone you want."

"Should we work on my telekinesis while we wait for the rendezvous time?" Sayah asked. "I feel like I could use more practice."

"Sure," Kage said. "What do you want to—" His voice cut off as she pulled the last slice of orange from his hand. "Really?"

"They are my favorite," she said, the laughter in her voice

bringing a smile to his face. "Besides, you hadn't eaten it yet and it's been sitting in your hand for at least twenty minutes." She shrugged.

Kage laughed and pulled her to him, wrapping his arms around her waist. Sayah put the slice of orange in her mouth and threaded her arms up behind his neck. Unexpectedly, Kage began to hum an off-key melody that struck a chord within her, drawing up a memory of watching her parents dance at a party from the railing at the top of the stairs. Kage began to sway in time to his humming, placing one of her hands on his shoulder and grabbing the other in his hand. He moved her with him until she began to follow him effortlessly, her natural grace aiding her in keeping time with the concerto he hummed for them. He spun her around in a circle, raising a surprised giggle from her throat.

"I've never danced before," Sayah said, resting her cheek against his chest as they swayed.

"I didn't think you had, but I couldn't resist the idea of dancing with you, especially when we don't know what will happen next. I didn't want to move forward without having a little piece of joy." Kage kissed her forehead and pulled her even closer in his embrace.

"I used to think I didn't deserve joy," Sayah whispered. "Watching my parents die…it felt as though my life was ripped away, too. I felt empty for years, barely surviving as I hid in the shadows of alleys and scavenged for food from the refuse piles behind taverns and inns. It seemed like I would never be whole again. But now—"

"Now you have Bess and me. A family, and something worth living for."

"Yes," she said. "And hope, which I haven't felt for a really, really long time."

"I'm glad," Kage said. He swayed her gently in time to

the song he had been humming, though he had stopped moments before. With a hand pressed into the small of her back, he dipped her slightly, then lifted her back up and spun her around again in dizzying circles. "If we make it out of this alive, if we defeat Dal'gon...I want you to stay with me."

"When we make it out of this alive and defeat Dal'gon, I would be honored to," Sayah said. "But only if you promise me something."

"What?" Kage asked.

"Promise me that you won't become power hungry like your father. That you're strong enough to withstand the demonic blood he gave you and just focus on being a good man, husband, and father." Sayah's face was serious.

"I promise." Kage dropped a feather light kiss onto her lips. "Did we ever get around to telling you how Dal'gon experimented on me?"

"No, you never did," she said.

"He injected me with angel blood when I was a small boy, putting it into my veins. Your mother's blood, spilled by Maddox on the street. I think that's why he's been so disappointed in me. He gave me the angelic blood I needed to become everything he hadhoped to create, but the blood wasn't enough to make me into what he wanted me to be." Kage shrugged. "In the end, the angelic blood curbed the base instincts that my demonic heritage should have increased, and I ended up with empathy and kindness, rather than the greed and lust for power he wanted."

"So he made you into who you are by using my mother's blood."

"Yes. Without her, I may not have turned out like this."

"I suppose, then, that one good thing did come out of her death. He experimented on you with her blood. But instead of becoming an even greater evil, you became a

good man, and I eventually met and fell in love with you."
Sayah leaned her cheek against his chest, listening to the
steady thrum of his heartbeat. "Thank you for telling me,"
she said.

Kage was quiet, holding her tightly. He rested his cheek
against the top of her head as they continued to sway.

Maddox saluted Dal'gon as he passed by his office on the
way out of the house. "I'll be back," he said. "I'm going out
to check out the Lyceum again, then heading up to Our Lady
of Charity to see if there have been any sightings of Sayah."

Dal'gon nodded dismissively and continued to study the
ledger before him. As Maddox walked out the door, he caught
the faint scent of fresh scones and lemon curd and turned
toward The Rusty Pig. Knocking on the kitchen door, he
smiled at Bess through the open upper half of the door.

"Hullo, Bess," he said. "Spare a scone or two for a
gentleman with an appetite?"

"As a matter of fact, I had just set aside a plate with a few
and some lemon curd in case a clever fellow such as yourself
wandered by to chat," she said flirtily, pulling her braid over
her shoulder as she looked up at him.

"Well, it's lucky I stopped by, then." He sat in the chair
beside the fireplace and snagged one of the scones from the
plate. Flecks of lemon zest and sanding sugar decorated the
surface of the delicate biscuit. "Any news?"

"He was by earlier today and dropped something for you.
You should be able to reach it if you stretch your hand down
between the hearthstones on the left."

"Are they safe?" he asked as he reached between the
stones to retrieve the small envelope tucked there.

"Yes, but anxious." Worry lined Bess's face. "It's to be tonight, isn't it?"

"Seems like it will be tonight, yes. We've run out of false leads to plant and Dal'gon's impatience could lead him to call some of the other disciples home to assist with the search. She is ready, so we need to make our move."

"You had better hope so, Maddox, or I'll have your hide once your father is through," Bess said, her voice bloodthirsty.

"I'll protect her, and Kage, to the best of my abilities." He smiled reassuringly and took another bite of scone. "I don't know if I've told you, but you're an absolute genius with scones."

"You have, almost every time you come here. Your brother says the same thing. But I'll never tire of hearing about it."

"Then I'll keep telling you," Maddox said. "But for now, I need to get running. I have to set up the capture before we put the plan in motion."

"Best of luck to you. All of you," Bess said. "When it's over and done, come here and I'll feed you lot."

"Beef pie?" Maddox asked with a grin.

Bess nodded and turned, snagging a scone off the baking sheet by the door and tossing it to him. He saluted her with it and ducked out the door, heading toward the sanctuary.

CHAPTER THIRTY-THREE

S ayah and Kage knelt in the far back of the Our Lady of Charity sanctuary, their heads bowed as they prayed with the priestess leading the service. The other churchgoers blocked them from view of the center aisle, hiding them in plain sight from any prying eyes in the crowd. Kage wrapped them in shadows as the blessing began and the worshipers moved toward the aisles to follow the path to the priestess and her acolytes at the front of the chamber. They slipped through a side door near the back of the sanctuary, entering the priestess's receiving room. The sounds of the crowd lessened as they grew further away.

"And now, I bring the blessing of Our Lady unto you," the priestess intoned, her voice echoing through the sanctuary. "May you be unworried and unharmed as you serve others in her name."

The crowd lingered, mingling amongst themselves as the priestess wandered through and greeted individual parishioners, chatting quietly with them. Sayah peered around the door, watching for Maddox and Reisu to appear.

"They should be here by now," Kage said, looking at the ornate clock on the wall.

"They'll be here." Sayah looked at the crowd as it slowly disbursed. "But if they aren't here before the rest of the crowd leaves, we'll need to move elsewhere. The priestess usually spends a few hours in this room after the last of the parishioners leaves. In quiet meditation, supposedly."

"Quiet meditation? Counting the coin from the collection basket, you mean?" Kage asked, disgust on his face as he remembered the silver marks he tossed into the basket. "Or maybe she's lacquering her toenails?"

Sayah shook her head, her shoulders shaking with mirth. "No idea, to be completely honest. I was never welcomed into this room after the services, but neither of those things would surprise me. The priestess and the acolytes typically left me alone, provided I was quiet and didn't cause any disruptions in the sanctuary."

Kage nodded, then stiffened suddenly. "Did you see that?"

"A shadow just moved on the back wall, but I can't be sure it wasn't just the light from the candle shifting. It's too far for me to get a good look." Sayah squinted, moving as close to the door's opening as she could. "It might be them. I saw a gray blur."

She moved back into the darkness to the left of the door, slipping behind Kage. The floorboards creaked and moaned softly under the weight of someone approaching them.

"Kage," Reisu whispered.

"Are we on schedule?" he asked.

"Yes," Maddox said as he released the shadows and embraced his brother. "Are you ready?"

Sayah nodded slightly, her face pale. She gripped Kage's

hand, fear tightening her throat. "You're sure this will work?" she asked Maddox.

"I'm sure. Do you need to grab anything before we go?"

"No. Everything I need is at the Pig for after—when we're done."

Maddox smiled. "Okay, to make this realistic, I'm going to have to bind you and carry you in. Reisu will lead Kage in behind us. We need to make it look like there was a struggle, though."

"Hit me," Kage said. He shook his head slightly as Maddox stared at him. "Hit me. Make sure you draw some blood or Father won't believe it." His head snapped back as Maddox's fist hit him in the mouth. Blood trickled down his chin, a bruise already forming around his split lip.

"Like that?" Maddox asked.

"You enjoyed that a little too much," Reisu said. "Let's get moving before the priestess gets in here and discovers us brawling in her office."

Maddox and Kage cloaked themselves in shadow and Reisu followed them out. Sayah paused as she left, lighting a candle along the sanctuary wall. "Our Lady, protect us," she whispered before twisting the shadows around herself and running after the others.

As they approached the dock district, Maddox released his shadows. Kage and Sayah followed suit and Sayah jumped as she felt the ropes of shadow wrap around her wrists, drawing them tightly together behind her back.

"I'm sorry," Maddox said as he hoisted her over his shoulder. "I feel like I keep having to do this. At least this time, it's for a good reason."

"It's okay. Let's just get this over with," Sayah said, squirming. She smiled at Kage reassuringly, then kicked her legs for good measure.

"Yes," Reisu said as she shifted into her corporeal form. "Make it look like you're struggling." She watched as Sayah shifted and tugged at the bindings behind her back. "That's perfect. Now Kage, come with me." She grasped his wrists in an iron grip, her thin fingers digging into his flesh, and pushed him forward to follow Maddox and Sayah.

The door to the brothel swung open by an unseen force as they approached. "Maddox," Dal'gon said, his voice booming from inside the house. "Bring them to me at once."

"Of course, Father," Maddox said. "Reisu, bring Kage to Father in his office. I will secure Sayah and get everything set up for the ritual."

Reisu nodded and pushed Kage through the door, passing Dal'gon to lead Kage into the office. Dal'gon lingered in the foyer, staring at Sayah as Maddox carried her, kicking and struggling, inside.

"Ensure that she is wearing the robe I have set out," Dal'gon said. "And find something to clean off that abominable scent that is lingering on her skin. I can't place it, but it makes me sick."

Kage flicked an amused glance at Maddox over his shoulder at his father's comment.

"I will do my best." Maddox squeezed her legs tightly together to keep her pinned against his shoulder and carried her up the spiral staircase. "Okay," he whispered. "So far, so good. Let's hope Kage is able to get the knife while Dal'gon is distracted."

"He will do it, he has to do it," Sayah whispered back. "He won't let me down."

As they crossed the threshold into Kage's childhood

bedroom, Maddox set her down gently and released the shadow bindings that had held her wrists. Sayah rubbed her wrists, massaging the stiffness from them.

"The robe?" she asked, studying the billowing pile of fabric strewn across the bed.

"Yes, that's the ritual robe he wants you to wear, he believes it will bring him luck." Maddox crossed to the armoire and grabbed the robe, a sheer black confection trimmed in delicate lace. He tossed it to Sayah, noting her grimace. "I know. You don't have to be fully nude; just put this on over your corset and bloomers. Make sure you don't have anything else under it," he said.

She nodded, reaching back to unlace her gown, then pulled it over her head. Once she wore the robe, Maddox led her to the chair at the center of the room and gently bound her around her waist, holding her to the chair but leaving plenty of space for her to move.

"Kage should be here soon," Maddox said. "Be as still as you can when Dal'gon comes in. Make sure he believes that you're truly restrained."

"I will." Sayah took a deep breath, trying to steady the nerves that caused her breath to thicken in her throat.

"You good?" he asked, noticing the pounding of her pulse in her throat. "Want to talk through the plan one last time?"

"Okay," she said. She inhaled, counting to five, then exhaled. "When Kage comes in, he'll give me the dagger. I'll slip out of the bindings and hide it…Where?"

"Where you think is best. Maybe on top of the armoire?"

"What about under the pillows on the bed? That should work," Sayah said, studying the pillows intently. "And then we have a second chance to use the dagger if something goes wrong."

"Good idea." Maddox sighed. "Now, let's go ahead and

make sure these bindings look realistic."

Maddox turned and walked out of the room, heading toward Dal'gon's office. Their raised voices greeted him as he approached the door.

"What do you mean, my foolish choices?" Kage shouted, anger painting his cheeks crimson as his blood pounded through his veins. "I brought her to you. I made sure you knew about her. I found her. No one else. Me."

"You found her, yes. You fell in love with her. You. You're more like your idiot mother than I thought. Always hoping and dreaming for things you can't have." He spat the words at Kage, malice filling his voice. "She doesn't love you, you fool. She just wants to be off the streets and you're a convenient way to achieve that. Once I make her my offer, she'll throw you over for me and you will get the hell out of my house." Dal'gon smiled, enjoying the pain that rippled across Kage's face at his assertions about Sayah.

"She will never accept you," Kage said. "Never."

Dal'gon laughed. "We shall see."

"Father," Maddox said, taking advantage of the brief lull in conversation to cut in. "She is ready. I ensured that she prepared for the ritual just as you requested. It is time for you to make your preparations for her."

"Ah, yes. My prize awaits." Dal'gon strode to the door, his booted feet echoing on the floorboards. "I shall go anoint myself in preparation for this blessed event. You will both have another sibling soon, and another disciple will join our ranks. My heir, who will topple governments and bring people to heel with a whisper." He motioned for Maddox to follow him, then locked the door.

"Send Reisu to me," he said quietly to Maddox after ensuring Kage was secured in the office. "I shall need her assistance in my preparations."

"Yes, Father."

A few moments later, Kage walked on quiet feet to the door, pressing his ear against it. The hallway was silent.

"Reisu," he whispered. "Are you here?"

Smoke billowed from the fireplace, forming itself into her curvaceous corporeal form. "I'm here," she said, her voice a low-pitched whisper. "Quickly, the key is in the marble urn to the left of the mantle, wrapped in shadow and suspended inside the lid."

Kage raced to the urn, lifting the lid gently and grabbing the key from its shadowy net. Sliding it into the lock on the desk drawer, he turned it carefully, holding his breath and listening for the satisfying click that indicated success. "Got it," he said. He slid the drawer open and took the dagger out, removing it from its sheath. Shoving it back in and placing the sheathed knife in his pocket, he locked the drawer and returned the key to its hiding spot.

"Go," Reisu said, pushing him toward the door to the hidden passageway. I'll close and lock the door, then come find you and Sayah. Dal'gon will be looking for me to help complete the anointing before he goes to her."

"Thank you," Kage said. "For everything."

"It's not the time for thanks. Just go. Let's end this." Reisu turned away and headed for the door, tossing a look at him over her shoulder. "There will be plenty of time for congratulations after this is over," she said before she shut and locked the door behind her.

Kage pushed the small lever at the back of the bookshelf, watching as one of the wooden panels on the walls slid free and shifted backwards. He ducked into the gap between the boards and slid the panel back into place, then darted through the narrow passage toward his bedroom.

"One, two... three. Here it is," he mumbled to himself as he counted the alcoves leading to the hidden doorway that led from the passage into his bedroom. He pressed the small lever and climbed through the opening into his room, then slid the door closed again. "Sayah," he said. "I'm here."

"Thank the gods," she whispered. "Do you have it?"

"Yes, right here. Can you get free?"

She shifted herself to the right and slid the band of shadow up over her shoulder, sliding down the side of the chair and freeing herself. Kage handed the dagger to her. She inspected it, turning it over in her hands.

"Amazing," she said, unsheathing the dagger and turning it over in her hands, "how such a simple looking thing can be the the end of such a powerful creature."

"Where are you going to hide it?" Kage asked.

"Right here," she said, lifting a pillow from his bed and slipping the dagger beneath it. "I was practicing while I waited. Hopefully this will work. If not...at least I'll be able to get the dagger when he tries to take me to bed."

"Sayah," Kage said, his face serious. "You don't—"

"I know, I can back out if I want to. But it's too late to turn back now, Kage. We can do this. We need to do this," she said. She pressed a kiss to his lips to silence his protests, then slid back into the chair and replaced the bindings around her chest. She twisted in the chair to look at him. "Quick, hide before Dal'gon gets here."

Kage slid underneath his bed and Sayah twisted shadows around him, obscuring him from view. "I love you," he whispered.

"I love you, too."

CHAPTER THIRTY-FOUR

Reisu massaged scented oil into Dal'gon's chest and abdomen, stroking his muscles with exactly the pressure he liked. The scent of dragon's blood and oud filled the air.

"Yes, perfect," he said as her hands kneaded his pectoral muscles. "That should be sufficient."

"You are ready?" she asked.

"I am ready." Dal'gon turned to the mirror, studying his oiled muscles as they glistened in the firelight. "Take me to my prize."

Reisu opened the door from Dal'gon's chambers and led him to Kage's room, her footsteps silenced by the thick Persian rug running down the center of the hallway. Maddox opened the door as they approached, stepping outside to hold it open to allow them to enter. He bowed before Dal'gon, the candlelight in the room glinting off of his bald head.

"Father," he said as he straightened. "She is ready for you."

Sayah struggled against her bindings, nearly tipping the

chair with her movements. "No," she screamed. "I won't do this. I am not ready for you. Let me go."

"Move her to the bed," Dal'gon said to Maddox, snapping the bindings around Sayah's waist with a gesture of his hand. He smiled at her, a feral gleam in his eyes.

She jumped up as the bindings fell away, diving for the door. Maddox grabbed her with a rope of entwined shadows and yanked her backward. Her bare feet slipped on the floor as she lost her balance and he caught her just before her head could slam into the heavy wooden post of the bed. He tossed her bodily onto the thick mattress. She sat up and scrambled backward, her back striking the heavy wrought iron of the headboard.

He loosened the ties at the waist of his breeches, allowing them to slip lower on his hips and exposing the thin trail of dark hair leading down from his belly button. "That won't be happening, he said. "You're mine, Sayah. You have been mine from birth."

"No, please," she pleaded, whimpering as he came closer to her. She flinched back from his hand as he reached out to touch her. "Don't." She cast her eyes downward and bit back a sob.

Dal'gon reached out to her again, this time stretching shadows, allowing the tendrils to drift across her skin. A crease formed between her eyebrows, but she held herself back and continued to feign fear and desperation as she waited for an opening. He continued to caress her with tendrils of shadow before putting his hands on her shoulders and pushing her back onto the bed. He grasped her thighs with his shadows and pulled her knees upward, spreading her legs before him and holding her in place. As he moved toward her, she reached for the power that dwelled within her heart and grasped it, stretching a shield around herself. The tendrils snapped back into Dal'gon, the impact startling him. She used her shadows to force him off of her and back from the bed. She pinned him to the wall with her powers, giving herself the space to stand back up.

"What the—" He cut off as a whip of shadow lashed across his face. Black blood bloomed from a cut below his eye.

"This is over," she said. Her eyes glowed with power and a golden aura shimmered around her, enveloping her body as the shield took full effect. She held out her hand and narrowed her eyes, glaring at Dal'gon. She twisted the shadows left and right, distracting him with lashes from every direction as she summoned the dagger.

Sayah's eyes narrowed in a focused glare, her lips twisted into a snarl. The pillow twitched slightly, almost unnoticeable to the naked eye, shifting just enough to allow the dagger free. She grabbed it from the air as it flew toward her and stabbed upward. The skin of Dal'gon's abdomen split open and she dragged the dagger upward, spilling his entrails. As he fell to his knees, she pulled the dagger from his body and smiled at him. He stared at her, watching as she thrusted it into his chest cavity. His breath caught in his throat and confusion filled his eyes.

"How... where..." he said as he fell to his knees.

"Hello Father," Kage said as he slipped free of Sayah's shadows and crawled out from under the bed. He dusted off his pants as he stood, a smirk on his face.

"You. You did this." Color fled from Dal'gon's face as he stared at his youngest son. "How did you find the key?"

"I did. But...not alone. Never alone," Kage replied, taking great pleasure in his father's confusion. "You are not as beloved among your disciples as you believe yourself to be. Goodbye Father."

Sayah slipped behind Dal'gon, the dagger held firmly in her hand despite the thick black blood congealed on its handle. She grabbed his forehead and pulled his head back, dragging the sharp instrument across his throat. With a final gurgle, Dal'gon fell forward, his face hitting the floor as his blood began to pool around him.

Sayah stepped over the corpse and into Kage's outstretched arms. With a sob, she dropped the dagger and rested her forehead against his chest. The rapid, angsty tears took them both by surprise, her body shaking with the strength of her sobs as she cried. Kage stroked her back, the cold sensation of her tears soaking his shirt a soothing balm to his heartache after hearing the woman he loved be tortured by his father. He pressed his lips to her forehead, blood and sweat marring the taste of her skin, then held her close. They comforted one another as the stress and pain of the past days caught up with them.

CHAPTER THIRTY-FIVE

S ome time later, Sayah undressed in a well appointed bedroom across the hall, having refused to stay in Kage's old room after Dal'gon was dispatched. Steam rose from the bathtub that stood before the brick fireplace, a cheerful fire crackling in the hearth despite the unseasonably warm fall weather. Every muscle in her body ached from weeks of sleeping on a measly pallet on the floor in the mildewed forecastle of the dry docked ship or squeezing herself into small spaces with Kage while they hid from Dal'-gon's disciples. She scrubbed the black blood from her hands and face at the washstand, removing all traces of Dal'gon's existence from them before she approached the bath.

We did it. We really did it, Sayah thought as she climbed into the huge copper soaking tub that the servants had hauled into the room. She sank into the hot water, slipping below the surface to wet her hair and face, then leaned back against the side of the tub and soaked her aching body. A small noise behind her caught her attention and she immediately threw up her invulnerability shield and whipped around, prepared to unleash her shadows. Kage uncloaked from the shadows and stripped off his clothes, dropping them in a pile atop the ruined corset and bloomers she had shed before entering the tub. He climbed into the tub with her and slid down until he was submerged up to his chin.

"Ah," he said. "This is bliss."

"Is it?" Sayah asked. "The tub is full of bloody water, despite my best efforts to get the majority of it off before I climbed in."

Kage smiled at her. "But it isn't our blood. It's blood that means you are safe and I am free."

She smiled. "You're right. I am safe now, and you are free. So are Maddox and Reisu."

"Free to do whatever we want," Kage said, a seductive tone in his voice. He grabbed her hand and pulled her onto his lap, running his free hand down her side. "Anything we want."

"Anything?" she asked.

"Anything."

She pulled his face toward her and kissed him deeply, teasing them both with strokes of her tongue against his. He moaned softly into her mouth, his hands gripping her hips. As he moved her astride him, she braced herself on the side of the tub. She kissed him again, distracting him until she could gain the leverage she needed to push him under the water. He abruptly resurfaced and found her giggling hysterically. He pushed his wet hair back from his forehead and attempted to give her a stern look.

"Well, you did say 'anything,'" she said innocently. "I thought we were due for some fun."

"Challenge accepted," Kage said. He grabbed her by the hips and lifted her onto him. "But first…"

Her giggles turned into a moan as he teased her to distraction.

The sound of water splashing was followed quickly by a rush of water from under the closed door into the hallway. Inside the room, giggles rang out, followed by a low moan. Maddox smirked as he walked by.

"They seem to be enjoying themselves," he said

"Very much so," Reisu said. "So why are we pacing the hallways instead of having some of our own fun?"

"Because," Maddox said. "Father's remains…"

She stopped abruptly and stared at him. "What about them?"

"They disappeared. The dagger, too."

"Surely not," Reisu said in disbelief.

"They did. I went back to dispose of them and they were gone." A shiver ran down Maddox's spine at the thought. "What are we going to do?"

Reisu sighed. "Research," she said. "We'll have to figure out what could cause that to happen. There aren't many records of demons being slain, but we will have to see what they say. In the meantime, don't tell your brother about this. Let him enjoy our victory and the chance to be with Sayah for as long as possible."

"I won't," Maddox said. "Eventually, though, we will need to tell them so that they can deal with whatever comes next."

"I agree. Eventually. Not today, or even next week, unless we discover something pressing."

"Okay. So…now what?" Maddox asked.

"Now you take me to bed," Reisu said. "Unless you'd rather get started researching what happens when a demon is slain."

Maddox grinned. "I'll take the first option."

She hiked her skirts up to her knees and took off at a run. "You'll have to catch me first," she shouted over her shoulder to him, laughter in her voice.

Maddox growled his appreciation as he started the chase.

Kage stroked Sayah's hair back from her face, pulling it free from the glow of sweat that coated her forehead. Half of the water from the tub was on the floor, but he couldn't find it in himself to care about the possible damage when she looked so delectable stretched out across the small dining table in the room. Her legs were spread and the pale skin of her thighs hugged his hips as he gazed down at her. He traced one fingertip around the bud of her taut nipple, then leaned forward and kissed her, nipping her bottom lip with his teeth.

"I love you," she said.

"I love you." He moved within her, finding the rhythm that sent them both spiraling over the edge. "Gods, how I love you."

She moaned in response and he felt her arch against him. He lifted one of her legs from its place around his hips and set her ankle on his shoulder, gripping her hips in his hands and lifting her to accommodate more of him.

"Oh gods, yes," she moaned.

"More?" he asked.

Sayah's eyes glazed over and her throat worked. She nodded, unable to get the words out, and dug her fingers into the muscle of his arms to steady herself as she melted under him. He kissed her, driving himself into her again and pushing them both over the edge. His arms wobbled and he collapsed, pressing her into the tabletop as his full weight crashed into her.

"Oof," she said with a giggle. "You're heavy."

"Sorry, love." He rolled off of her and stood, pulling her with him.

Sayah rested her head on his shoulder and nuzzled her cheek against his chest. "We did it," she said.

"We did," Kage said, dropping a kiss onto her forehead. "We did."

CHAPTER THIRTY-SIX

Damon had to ensure that Dal'gon would survive the brutal attack. It was the only way that he could ensure his return to the disciples. He lurked outside the door to Kage's bedroom, listening as the betrayers discussed their next move and celebrated their victory over the Master, waiting for them to leave the room. He hid himself in the alcove outside an adjoining room, listening to their footsteps as they exited the room and walked down the hallway in the other direction. He snuck through the door and stood over Dal'gon's lifeless body, terror and grief clogging his throat.

He ripped a hole into the shadow realm and shifted into shadows. In the darkness, he became a pale light that shifted through the shadows carrying a prone body. The shadow realm was rife with danger when you entered without Dal'-gon's permission, but Damon knew that it was worth the risk of crossing him to save his life. Distant shrieking filled the air as he traversed the rocky path from the entrance of the realm. The path forked and he followed it to the left, heading to the one place capable of performing the miracle he hoped to achieve: the reflecting pools.

He entered the valley that held the reflecting pools and carefully laid Dal'gon's corpse in the water. Ripples disturbed the black surface as the body floated, shining bright in the darkness, as though the water radiated light despite the unending blackness surrounding it. Magic filled the air.

He knelt, opening his pack and removing a crumbling book. "Might as well give this a shot," he said. He carefully turned the wrinkled pages, finding the ancient words of revival in the water stained pages of the text. "Shadow made flesh, strength unmatched. Spirit, blood, and bone, restore what was taken. Make his body whole, return breath to his lungs." He watched in anticipation, willing Dal'gon's chest to rise and fall with breath again.

"Nothing," Damon said after several minutes had passed. Frustration and disappointment filled him as he watched the corpse drift back to shore. "Gods damn it, I can't do anything ri—"

A muscle in Dal'gon's face twitched slightly, then his lips parted to take a breath. He sat up and opened his eyes. Damon jumped at the unexpected movement.

"Master," Damon shouted, elated at the sight of Dal'gon. "You have returned to us."

"Fool," Dal'gon's corpse said, its lips barely moving. "You mess with magic far greater and more dangerous than you know. What you have just released will be the end of civilization." The reanimated corpse fell back to the ground beside the reflection pools, still.

Damon stared at the corpse, shadows twisting around it from the water of the pools. A great whooshing noise echoed through the shadow realm as a cloaked figure dove at Damon. Gooseflesh rose on his arms as a chill ran down his spine.

The being lunged, wrapping itself around him and sinking into his flesh. He shuddered as the shadows disappeared into him, then watched as the reflecting pools reached up and sucked Dal'gon's body underwater. Only a few bubbles remained where his corpse had floated on the edge of the shore. In the distance, maniacal laughter sounded, echoing throughout the shadow realm.

Damon scrambled backward from the reflecting pools, catching a glimpse of himself in the water. His normally pudgy features were smooth and thin, the pock marks on his cheeks erased by whatever shadowy pact he had made. Long black hair hung down toward his shoulders in gentle waves, and his eyes, always a shade of brown that reminded him of rich, dark coffee, were now the color of a turbulent ocean under the night sky.

"What? How…" He took a deep breath, pondering the question. "What did I do by trying to resurrect Dal'gon?"

The shadow realm seemed to laugh again as it tossed him out, sending him flying into the abyss. The being that lurked inside him grinned.

EPILOGUE

I hunger, the being thought into Damon's mind. *We must feed, and soon.* Damon brushed the hair back from his face and peered around the corner toward the brothel. He sent tendrils of shadow out, feeling along the walls to check for wards and booby traps. Using the shadows, he crept out of the alley, stepping into the safe spaces he located and inching closer toward the back door of the brothel. He swore under his breath as the door swung open and two of the girls walked down the back steps. One of them, a lovely brunette with petite features and large breasts, lit a cigarette and held it between her crimson lips, inhaling deeply.

Her, Damon thought as he stared at her. The other being in his head growled its agreement and reached for control of his body. Damon resisted. *No,* he thought. *We must be patient and wait for them to be separated. Then we will feast.* Beside him, a shadow twisted into the form of a man with horns like a crown atop his head. The creature shook its head in disagreement, but Damon stared it down, pushing it back into himself. *Wait.*

The other girl, a voluptuous redhead with a curvaceous

pair of buttocks and cleavage that could smother a man, took the cigarette from the brunette and held it aside. She pulled her friend close to her, taking her lips in a passionate kiss. As they ground their bodies against one another, the smaller brunette fondled the redhead's buttocks, squeezing them and pulling her closer. The cigarette fell to the ground, smoldering, while Damon watched them in voyeuristic pleasure.

The redhead whispered something into the brunette's ear and they giggled. With a smack on her rear, the redhead ran up the stairs, playfully tossing her hair back over her shoulder as she winked at her friend. The brunette lit another cigarette and took a long drag.

Damon crept forward again and flicked out a thin string of shadow, knocking the cigarette away from her. He swung it back around, grasping her wrist and pulling her toward him. As he reeled her in, he stuffed a gag of shadow in her mouth, silencing her to ensure that she couldn't cry out.

"Hello," he said as she reached him. He grasped her wrist in an iron grip and smiled. "There is someone I'd like you to meet."

As he shifted into his other form, he released the gag and fed on her delicious screams as he ripped into her flesh.

ACKNOWLEDGMENTS

Being a creative soul is difficult and thankless at the best of times. I would not be where I am today without Ebony Norwood-Brown and Cassandra L. Thompson, my amazing editors. Likewise, every writer has their dearest writing friends who lift them up and valiantly fight imposter syndrome by their side—I don't know what I would do without the brilliant K.R. Wieland, who always picks me up when I'm at my lowest with a kind word and gentle encouragement.

To my husband Mick—thank you for all of the countless meals, water refills, and snuggle sessions that got me through the umpteen drafts of this book. I am so lucky to have a partner who supports my desperate need to craft stories and doesn't mind binge watching one of my comfort shows while I work on the countless edits I push myself through. I genuinely could not write without you by my side cheering me on. Es tevi mīlu.

To my children, who never complain about listening to me ramble on about plot points and character sketches at the dinner table—thank you for everything, especially all the hugs and ice cream breaks. I love you.

To Skylar, my best friend and heterolifemate—thank you for letting me send you some of the spicier scenes in this book so that I could have honest, hilarious feedback.

To Aunt Cindy—thank you for always believing in me. I don't think I will ever be able to adequately tell you how much I appreciate your unending support. I am so proud to be your niece and so grateful for everything you have done for me. Love you!

Last, but certainly not least, to Mémère, my beloved grandmother who we lost in February 2022. Thank you for always being my biggest fan and supporter. I know you are looking down on me, bragging to God and the angels about your granddaughter. I love you.

ABOUT THE AUTHOR

Tiffany Putenis holds a Masters degree in English and Creative Writing from Southern New Hampshire University. Her love for the written word started at an early age, and she continues to be fascinated by works of fiction. Her favorite stories in recent years have been high fantasy, but she still has a healthy love of vampires that started in high school when she discovered Bram Stoker and Anne Rice. She works as a freelance editor and assists with acquisitions for Quill and Crow Publishing House in addition to writing her own works of fiction. Tiffany lives in the American Northeast with her husband, three kids, and 2 cats. When she isn't writing, she finds solace in hiking through the beautiful forests that surround her home.

You can find Tiffany on:

 twitter.com/PutenisWrites

 instagram.com/TPutenisWrites

 tiktok.com/@tputeniswrites